Heart of the Spirit Man

A NOVEL BY GEORGE MENDOZA

WISE TREE PRESS
Mesilla Park, New Mexico

To my daughter,

Maria G. Mendoza

Author's Note

In 2011, I had a terrible hiking accident in the Organ Mountains in New Mexico where I live and dream my dreams. I fell a good thirty feet, broke my arm and my teeth. I suffered from cluster headaches for a long time after that fall.

I was lucky to be alive but the cluster headaches were terrible. I saw vivid visions which I painted and which turned into this story about Michael Spiritman. The headaches and pain somehow led to a wildly productive period during which I painted up a storm and wrote novels about my superhero, the spirit man.

One day the clusters stopped but I continued to paint and write books. I guess it's true that a good bump on the head can bring out the creativity! I have been accused of living in a fantasy and dreaming my life away. That's probably true, and I would not have it any other way.

Heart of the Spirit Man is the third in the series, following *Journey of the Spirit Man* and *Vision of the Spirit Man.*

Acknowledgements

I would like to express my deep appreciation to Erne Barge, Dr. David Boje, Amy Brainard, Louie Burke, the Castillo family, my art teacher, Imelda Chacon, Bobby Cook, Mayra Enriquez, my sister Kathleen Firth, Dick Guttman, Janus Herrera, Neal Hidalgo, Anne Hillerman, Craig Holden, Dr. Dan Howard, Sonny Irizarry, Thomas Kindig, Doylene Land, Daniel Landes, Jamie Lapage, Michael Marrufo, James McConnell, Melanie McQuiddy, my son, Michael Mendoza, J.L. Powers, Beth Ramp, Robert Rivera, Jennifer Romero, Ron Rowlett and his son Ryan Rowlett, Antonio Sanchez, Jane Seymour, Mary Sherman, Holly Watson, Vernon Wilson, Thomas Zubia and others who wish to remain anonymous.

I am very grateful to James Salas and Raquel Ortega with the New Mexico Commission for the Blind who funded this incredible book project. To Jessica Powers and Kathy McInnis who designed this beautiful book. To my agent, Frank Weimann, Folio Literary Management, New York. And to my editor, Shane Inman, the man with the magic touch!

— continued —

A special thanks to New Mexico State University, the NMSU English Department and especially the Creative Writing staff for their help and support in this and other projects.

All characters in this book are figments of my imagination with the exception of Michael Spirit Man.

George Mendoza
New Mexico

Chapter 1

Michael Seymour had been running when his heart stopped. On an ordinary evening, striding easily past the chaparral and the yucca deep-shadowed as the last desert rays wafted gray over the mountainous horizon, something broke. It was as if a hand from some other world reached into the fleshy lattice of Michael's chest and squeezed. He stumbled at first, putting a hand to his breast as the vice tightened, expecting the pressure to ease a moment later. But the hand only squeezed harder. As dusk slipped soundlessly into night, Michael fell.

What followed were only slashes. A knife tearing through the black cloth of oblivion here and there to reveal flashes of time, of life, of the world that was fast slipping away. Someone shouting. Hands rolling him onto his back. Blurry and indistinct faces that seemed desperately far away despite being mere inches from his own. More pressure. His sternum cracking. Sirens. Lights. The rattling, bouncing motion of the back of a vehicle like a ship in storm. Electricity surging through his body once, twice, three times as some distant voice cried, "Clear! Clear!"

Then the knife grew too dull and the darkness became all-encompassing.

Spirit Man sat up from the operating table. He glanced down and winced at the grisly scene beneath him—Michael's physical form as pale as death, a mask pumping anesthetic into his lungs. None of the surgeons or nurses appeared to notice Spirit Man yet, but he wasn't about to give them time to. He slipped from the table and stealthily exited the operating room, leaving behind that man who both was and was not him, who tethered this dream form to the real world and gave purpose to his long, long life.

"I'll be back," he whispered as he left. "I'll find whoever did this to you."

The hospital hallway was nearly deserted. Machines beeped and whirred and the smell of disinfectant made Spirit Man dizzy. He felt himself becoming more real, more tangible as he walked. That wouldn't do. If anyone saw him wandering about in this flimsy hospital gown, they'd stick him in one of the dreary, sterile rooms he passed and lock the door. He'd be no help to Michael like that. Footsteps echoed around a corner just ahead and without any time to think, he darted into the nearest room. One bed was empty, but in the other lay an old, old woman idly watching a soap opera on the TV. Damn. She looked at him quizzically as he cast about for somewhere to hide from the approaching footsteps. No dice.

The footsteps were almost to the door now, and he could hear two women talking.

"Are you going to Marlene's party?" said one.

"Depends. Do I have to wear a costume?" said the other.

"Oh, come on. Everyone's going to be wearing one! Isn't that the whole point of Halloween?"

"Ugh, fine, I'm sure I can throw something together."

"When are you off?" said the first voice. They were right outside the door now and, to Spirit Man's horror, seemed to have stopped moving.

"Gotta check on Mrs. Everton and then I'm off."

Damn again. Without any better ideas, he dashed to the far side of the room and lay down on the floor beside the old woman's bed, out of sight of the door. She pushed herself up and peered at him again and he just put a finger to his lips. She smiled, winked, and lay back down. The door opened. The footsteps drew near.

"How are we tonight, Mrs. Everton?" said the nurse.

"Oh, just lovely," the old woman said.

"I'm so glad. Do you need anything before I clock out?"

"Not a thing, dear. You go on and have yourself a fun night. Maybe tomorrow I'll tell you a story or two about my partying days."

The nurse laughed. "Well, you have a good night then."

A moment later she was gone. Spirit Man let out a long tense breath, and stood.

"Uh, thanks," he said.

"Don't mention it, young man," said Mrs. Everton. She grinned. "Handsome fellow like you ought to be better at dodging the ladies by now."

He blushed, thanked her again, then poked his head out the door to make sure the coast was clear. When he was sure it was, he closed Mrs. Everton's door gently behind him and padded down the hallway, keeping his eyes wide open for anything that might help him escape the hospital undetected. As if in answer to his prayers, he spotted a supply closet. He ducked inside and, after a moment of fumbling, found and clicked on the light switch.

"Bingo."

There in front of him was a stack of neatly-folded janitor jumpsuits. He stripped out of his hospital gown and pulled on one of the brown jumpsuits. There was a name tag on the left front pocket. Oddly enough, it read "SPIRIT MAN." Well. Somebody must have been expecting him.

Outfitted with his fresh disguise, he strolled through the hospital like he owned the place. His friend Lohman worked as a janitor, and had once told him, "Nobody who thinks himself important ever pays attention to people who push a mop for a living." He hoped his friend was right. For good measure, he grabbed a trash bag off a cleaning cart as he passed. It was definitely a handy prop for someone looking for the exit.

As he passed the staff lounge, a rowdy group on their way to the hospital's Halloween party passed by, all dressed up in costumes. Doctors and nurses had become clowns, witches, vampires with faces painted a ghastly white. Considering the business conducted by a hospital, it all seemed a little ghoulish to him, but he wasn't about to start an argument, given his current predicament. He had a strange sense that he'd seen all of them before, and at the same time felt that he'd never met any of them at all. He'd have to figure that out later. He gave them all a friendly nod and a smile, more than a little worried they might immediately notice he wasn't one of the usual cleaning crew, but they barely acknowledged him at all. Not even a second glance. Guess Lohman was right after all.

At last, he found a door marked STAIRS and pushed through into a stairwell drenched in the sickly green light of old fluorescents. He walked down several flights of stairs to the ground floor and finally there it was: the exit. Just a few more seconds and he'd be free. But just as he started to breathe a sigh of relief, who should cut between him and the door but another janitor? He stopped short, sure he was about to be busted...until the janitor turned to face him and flashed a wry smirk.

"Lohman!" Spirit Man said. "Man, am I glad to see you."

"C'mon," Lohman said, nodding toward the door. "Let's get you outta here."

They emerged onto a small cement stoop beside the unmarked staff entrance. Spirit Man took a deep, grateful breath of the open air, glad to be free of the powerful air conditioning in the hospital, which left the place feeling stuffy, almost suffocating. As soon as they were out in the cool night, Lohman pulled a cigarette from his pocket and lit it. He leaned against the wall of the hospital and took a long drag before offering the carton to Spirit Man.

"Want one?" he said.

"Thanks, but I'll pass. I hear they're bad for the heart."

Lohman chuckled. His laugh, like his voice, was deep and slow—tectonic plates shifting beneath Spirit Man's feet.

"Yeah, I understand you've got yourself a bit of a problem," Lohman said.

"You could say that." Spirit Man's hand went instinctively to his own chest. "Do you have any idea what could've caused it?"

Lohman squinted across the parking lot. The lot was almost entirely still and dark. Most of the stars were drowned out by the light of the hospital but the lights of the city glimmering in the distance were almost as good. Far overhead the moon beamed down a flat, shadowless light and the face on its surface gazed down at the men with blank, unfeeling eyes. Stone eyes.

"You're asking the wrong question," Lohman said.

"I'm not following."

"It's not a question of what. It's a question of who."

"You mean someone stopped Michael's heart on purpose? Who would do that?"

Spirit Man's mind raced. He had plenty of enemies in the dream world of Shook, but none who could reach across the veil to the waking world. Or so he thought.

"Can't say," Lohman said. He stubbed out his cigarette. "One thing I do know? There's a whole world of trouble waiting for you up ahead."

"Yeah, I had a feeling." Spirit Man rubbed his temples. "Well, guess I'd better get to it."

"Guess you had. Good luck, Spirit Man. And be careful. It's a cold world out there."

Spirit Man nodded. What was there to say to that? He stuffed his hands in his pockets and walked away from the hospital, leaving Lohman behind. He paused only once, at the far end of the parking lot, to look back at the hospital. Only a few lights shone from the windows. And somewhere inside, Michael waited for Spirit Man to save him.

Spirit Man crossed Telshor Boulevard without seeing a single car on the street. So strange, for there to be no one out and about on Halloween. He went up University Avenue a block or two, then made a turn onto a dirt road which led into the desert. He couldn't say exactly why he chose this path, only that something in his chest urged him along it. A sort of internal compass directing the way. He walked quickly and steadily, bracing himself for what was to come. More violence, to be sure. More strife. But there was nothing he wouldn't do to protect Michael. Not one solitary thing.

Soon, the desert road became a narrow trail winding up a steep hill he knew as Mount Solitaire. He climbed it quickly, with little exertion, and looked for the glinting lights of Las Cruces far below. But the city, so recently aglow, was dark, invisible in the night. Something wasn't right. He turned his eyes skyward and saw that the stars, too, were dark, despite the lack of clouds in the sky. Even the moon was dimmer than it had been moments before. A cold wind ripped across the mountain and he shivered.

He kept walking, following the compass needle in his chest. The real world began to seem far away. A dark forest of tall pines loomed in front of him. There were no forests near the hospital. The feeling of shifting realities, shifting planes, was so smooth to him now that he didn't even notice it, but surely he wasn't in his old world anymore.

And all for the better, as far as he was concerned. The answer to Michael's condition lay not in Michael's world, but in Spirit Man's. As he picked his way through the dense undergrowth (which belonged more to the Pacific Northwest than the desert of New Mexico), he tried to push out the rest of the "real world" out of his mind. The more he let go of that physical plane, the thicker the forest grew. He would soon be lost if his internal compass suddenly failed, but he didn't care. Somewhere ahead lay Michael's salvation. That was the only thing in the universe that mattered.

Chapter 2

The gigantic pine trees swayed in a harsh wind, far colder than it ought to have been in October. Spirit Man pulled the collar of his jumpsuit tighter with a shiver. The wind rushed through the tall pines and moaned balefully as he walked along the narrow path through the enchanted wood. He was glad he'd found the jumpsuit, especially as he stuffed his hands deeper in his pockets and imagined how much colder he would be if he were still wearing that woefully thin hospital gown. Though, of course, he was, in a sense. However far he got from Michael, he was still connected to the young man in spirit, still as much the same person as they were separate beings.

The tops of the trees towered hundreds of feet above him, a million dew-dropped pine needles glistening and sparkling in the waning moonlight. Where was the spirit world taking him?

Around another bend, he came to a small clearing, where stood a huge yellowish rock, an ochre monolith over two hundred feet tall, rising up through the towering pines. Dark blood dripped down the jagged surface of the huge rock, glistening in the moonlight as if it was still wet. Was Spirit Man alone here? He looked back through the trees but their branches and the underbrush had tangled together, barring any possibility of retreat. He was supposed to be right where he was and there was no going back. It even seemed like the bushes were growing out toward him, pressing into his back and the backs of his legs and urging him close to the stone platform. Spirit Man stepped forward cautiously, all his senses alert for any sign of an attacker.

Then something caught his attention. Something on the wind. Each gust seemed to carry with it the faint sound of drunkenness and music fading in and out, a warbling, swirling of distant sounds, like fragments snatched from songs or the cheering of crowds, tumbling together like falling autumn leaves. He strained to make out the sounds or their source. There had been no one since he'd left the hospital, certainly not since he had entered the forest. Nothing alive but him, it had seemed. Where could those sounds be coming from? He looked back into the trees, willing his eyes to peel back the darkness, but still he couldn't get any good sense of where the sounds were coming from. The wind and the trees distorted the sounds of revelry and made it sound like the partiers were everywhere, all around him, closing in. Still he could see nothing, and he stepped fully into the clearing, not wanting to be surprised by anything that might be lying in wait in the undergrowth. Then, with a little gasp, like the whole world had just sucked in its breath, the forest fell absolutely silent.

Spirit Man's whole body tensed to fight or run, waiting for something to move, for whatever this world had waiting for him. Even the wind in the trees had vanished. In the overpowering quiet, Spirit Man could hear his own heartbeat.

Then, softly, graceful as a mountain lion, a man dropped from some hidden crag on the immense rocky plinth and landed on the opposite end of the clearing. He raised himself to his full height, revealing himself to be at least seven feet tall, broad across the chest with arms thick as the trees around them. How could someone so large move so quietly? The stranger wore a long royal blue robe, flowing like a stream of wind over the ground as he walked in measured steps across the clearing, around the yellow stone. Spirit Man didn't move, waiting to see what he wanted, what he would do. The man wore a golden mask like something out of an ancient Greek tragedy. From the sides of the mask flashed arcs of electricity a few inches long, sparking and crackling, as if they were emerging from his very temples. His hair was long and even in the moonlight, it shone like gold in the New Mexico sun as it cascaded upon his muscular shoulders. Through the eye-holes in the mask, his eyes blazed with a terrible promise. But a promise of what?

Still, Spirit Man remained poised, ready, a deep uneasiness curling in his gut. Finally, with a deep and smooth voice, the man spoke.

"Don't be afraid, Spirit Man. Your adventure is about to begin!" He gave a rumbling chuckle. His voice was familiar in the way that the desert is always familiar, whenever you wander into it. It was as if the stranger had a primordial voice, like he spoke from the ages beyond time, beyond any world Spirit Man had ever known. And Spirit Man had known many worlds.

"All right. Who are you?" Spirit Man said. He kept his tone respectful, neutral. It was never a good idea to anger strangers, especially in the spirit worlds, when anyone could be nearly anything.

"I am Lord Striker, of the dream world of Shook," the man said. He paused a moment, waiting for recognition to sink in.

Spirit Man knew the name, but his memory of it was hazy. The name lay at the bottom of a deep well and he couldn't quite see through the murky waters. All he knew was that nothing good was associated with such a name.

Lord Striker tilted his head back as though sizing up Spirit Man. Then he smiled a long-toothed smile.

"I have something to show you, Spirit Man."

The calm of his tone made Spirit Man's blood run cold. He bent his knees softly, readying himself to jump or run or launch forward into this menacing stranger if he had to.

"What if I say no?" he said.

"I don't think you will. It pertains to a mutual friend. One Michael Seymour."

Spirit Man's heart skipped a beat. Not a what, but a who, Lohman had said. This, then, must be that "who."

"What have you done?" Spirit Man said. He realized his fists were clenched, his nails digging into his palms.

"Follow me and you'll find out."

Then, with all the shocking grace with which he had arrived, Lord Striker leapt into the air and grabbed hold of a ledge on the stone pillar. He launched himself upward, grabbed another handhold, and continued like this, bounding up the sheer rock face with speed and agility that would be astonishing if exhibited by a man half his size, but which became downright unbelievable in a man of his build.

Spirit Man cursed under his breath and began to follow. The cliff loomed over him, seeming to taunt him as he made his ascent. He reached carefully from one handhold to the next, holding tight to the rock with all the strength his fingers could offer. Lord Striker had long since disappeared over the lip of the bluff. By the time he was halfway up, Spirit Man's arms ached and his legs burned. He hazarded a glance below him and immediately wished he hadn't. The ground lay at least a hundred feet below and there was nothing to stop his fall if he should slip. His vision swam. He closed his eyes for a moment, steadied himself, and resumed his climb.

Finally, after what felt like hours, Spirit Man clambered to the top of the cliff and threw himself onto the flat surface he found there. It was as if this platform had been erected for just such an occasion. The top of the pillar was perfectly round and perfectly flat, a sort of ritual altar jutting high into the night sky. After huffing and puffing for a minute, Spirit Man hauled himself to his feet. And there, in the center of the platform, he saw Michael. Michael lay on his back, still asleep, still draped in his hospital gown. Spirit Man rushed to his side and knelt down to check his pulse. He was still alive, thankfully.

"What have we gotten ourselves into this time?" Spirit Man said.

He turned to face Lord Striker.

"What did you do?"

"I do apologize, Spirit Man," Lord Striker said. Then, in a flash too fast to follow, he leaped through the air and pounced, throwing Spirit Man down to the ground. In that instant, Spirit Man sank back into Michael's body and the two were one again. Michael choked out a gasp as the breath was knocked out of him. Lord Striker pinned him down on his back, and though Michael and Spirit Man tried to squirm, it was like having a huge slab of stone pressing down on them. The wind picked up once more and came rushing from all sides at once, and a cloud of smoke and dust swirled up into the sky around them. Michael tried to cry out but the dust and the weight pressing down on him choked him until he coughed.

Lord Striker drove his knees into Michael's abdomen and spread apart his helpless arms. Michael tried again to yell but all he could manage was a pitiful gasp. Then Lord Striker opened his mouth and growled with the ferocity of a mountain lion, exposing a mouthful of six-inch long, razor-sharp white fangs. Saber teeth flashing in the bright moonlight, Lord Striker leaned down close, his teeth a hair's breadth from Michael's neck.

"I hate to be rude, Michael Seymour," he said, still in that same calm, ancient voice. "But you have something I need."

Michael's eyes widened with panic. Not even the mighty Spirit Man could break out of Lord Striker's grasp.

There was a scalding heat at Michael's wrists as Lord Striker's hands transformed into the massive paws of an enormous grizzly bear, covered with dark golden tangled fur and bearing brutally sharp claws. Michael tried to jerk an arm free, but Lord Striker held him fast and roared so forcefully, Michael thought he might go deaf. Blood ran down his arms where the bear's claws dug into them.

With razor-sharp teeth, the golden bear tore the janitor's uniform and the hospital gown beneath, exposing Michael's bare chest. Then, with a savage thrust, Lord Striker jammed his claws into the center of Michael's chest and wrenched his rib cage apart. Finally, he reached deep into the chest cavity, wrapped both paws around the bloody pounding heart, and ripped it out.

Michael had never felt such pain in his life. His head flashed with memories, all the lives he'd lived and all the lives he'd left behind—the terrible coliseum of Gehenna, the beauty of the badlands rejuvenated by Shook's healing power, the dying rattles of the diners falling before a wild gunman. So many memories of violence, of wonder, of love and loss. So many places he'd left behind. He would escape to any one of them now if he could, just to be free of this pain. His breath slowed and he gave a soft gasp, staring up into the cold and starless sky above and praying for a single glimmer of light. None appeared.

Lord Striker, covered in Michael's blood, stood once more to his full height. He was no longer a bear, nor was he a man. He looked like something in between, some awful hybrid creature that had never been meant to walk this land. Throwing back his blue cape, he held the heart in his huge bear-like hands and considered it with a level expression. Still it beat, a gentle but strong rhythm. Lord Striker brought it close to his face and smiled faintly.

Then, with a horrid rattlesnake tongue, Lord Striker licked Michael's heart. The forked tongue, pink and fleshy and prehensile, caressed the heart for just an instant before it recoiled back between lips smeared red with blood. Michael watched this as if from afar, feeling the life force quickly drain from his body. The gaping hole in his chest seemed obscene, impossible, and yet still he lay there, gasping gently now that his airway was no longer restricted. He ought to have been dead and yet he knew without a shadow of a doubt that he was alive, knew because the pain in his chest burned like the gaping, bloody wound had been filled with hot coals. He wanted to stand up and run, he wanted to scream out the pain in his heart, but he lacked the strength to do either. He could still feel it, the missing organ, even as he could see with his own eyes that Lord Striker held it in his clawed hands. He could feel the cold wind blowing over it, feel the terrible and tender sense of it being out in the open, the strangeness of being undefended for the first time. He could feel the rough pads of Lord Striker's hands on the wet muscle, and he shuddered at the sensation.

Lord Striker raised Michael's beating heart up to the dim moon and for a brief moment the moon bloomed red, dripping down from the sky above, dripping down to settle behind the trees, flowing down behind the horizon. Michael's blood dripped upon Lord Striker's gold-masked face and Striker began to chuckle, low in his throat, a sound like an avalanche in the distance until it grew into a booming laugh that filled the clearing. Michael's hands trembled and he felt as if there was still an invisible force pressing down on him, holding him to the ground. His vision blurred, his head ached horribly. The smoke in the air seemed to swirl into faces sneering down at him; Wendy crying tears of blood; Mark's gasping shock as his life spilled onto the dirt. All the bloodshed of his past returned to the present and formed shackles around his wrists and ankles, keeping him down.

                    HEART OF THE SPIRIT MAN

Lord Striker's laughter finally died and he shook Michael's heart in the air, droplets of blood spattering Michael's body. Michael's blood ran between Striker's long fingers and onto the ground by his feet, black with the night, pooling in tiny hollows, splattering the black-polished boots of the golden-haired giant from Shook. The cuffs of his royal blue robe were wet and gleaming with blood.

"Spirit Man, I thought you would put up more of a fight," Lord Striker said. "Where's your fighting spirit? I hold your heart in my hand and all you can do is gape at me? Of course you had no chance of defeating me—me, Lord of Shook—but I'll admit I expected more from you. Ah well. Life is so full of little disappointments, as you well know." He turned the still-beating heart in his hands greedily, almost reverently. But was there a hint of something else there? Some half-forgotten melancholy?

"This is mine, now," Lord Striker told Michael in a calm voice. Michael shuddered. His voice was like a rumble of thunder, the crack of his words lightning in the air. "This muscle, this meat. It's mine." He stooped and picked up a chunk of yellow stone the size of his fist, which had broken off the rocky platform during their struggle. Lord Striker tossed the hunk of stone into Michael's gaping chest cavity and Michael gave a gasping, shocked sound. It felt like he'd been hit by a car.

"For your trouble," Lord Striker said with a dark chuckle. "Everything in balance, you know."

Striding back and forth with steps so long and smooth he seemed to be gliding, Striker faced the red moon with a rumbling sigh. He did look regal, standing there on the mountaintop, shaking his long hair from side to side as he looked north and south. With a flourish, he pulled, seemingly from the air, an intricately engraved crystal decanter. On each side was a sweeping curved silver handle, a single piece of gleaming metal which also firmly held on the crystal stopper in place. Lord Striker opened the vessel and dropped Michael's heart inside. Only it didn't hit the bottom, it remained suspended without touching any of the decanter's walls, floating as if on strings.

As soon as the heart entered that crystal container, Michael felt as if the wind had been knocked out of him and he would never breathe again. Where previously he had felt the heart, felt everything that touched it, now it was simply gone. Vanished. No longer a part of him at all. He didn't feel the crystal of the decanter, didn't feel the cool air within, didn't feel anything.

"I suppose you'll come after me, Spirit Man," Lord Striker said, "dragging your little pet Michael along for the ride. All the better."

Spirit Man...Wasn't that only Michael? Why was Lord Striker speaking of them as two separate people? Were they? God, his chest hurt....He coughed weakly, trying to flex his fingers, trying to move around the heavy weight of the stone in his chest. He looked down and saw that his bones and muscle and skin were gradually knitting themselves back together, sealing the stone in that dark cavity where his heart ought to have been.

"No," he croaked, reaching to stop the healing. "No."

But he was too weak. His chest closed itself over the hunk of rock.

Striker laughed with dark amusement and shook the decanter and the heart thumped against the glass with a sickening squelch.

"Just know this," Lord Striker said. "When you do, inevitably, pursue me, I will kill you. And if you come back to life, I will kill you again. And again. And as many time as it takes. This heart will never be yours again. I will make certain of it."

Lord Striker swirled his cape around himself, off the pillar of stone, and disappeared.

Chapter 3

For a long time, the altar atop Mount Solitaire was silent. The night was infinite and dawn was an impossibility. Finally, movement. A haze began to gather about the platform and swirl slowly. It thickened and spread, rising up as a gray cloud bank which swelled to cover the entire mountaintop. The sky grew darker as the swirl became a gale, and the clouds began to surge and churn. The trees sighed and swayed against one another at first, and then began to creak and groan as tiny branches were ripped from them to join the swirling, frenetic chaos of wind encircling Michael.

Michael lay like the gutted sacrifice to some ancient god, blood drying on the hard rock around him. The pain in his chest had settled into a dull ache, steady and constant and without rhythm. The stone lay heavy behind his newly mended ribcage and he felt he might never be able to rise with it holding him down. The swirling winds rose up from him, and the clouds above arched high over the mountaintop. Great nimbus masses joined at their crowns to form a huge cathedral, with walls as dark as raging smoke. His body began to shudder, as though every muscle fiber in the limp flesh had begun to twitch, as the earth beneath it shook in seismic awe of the gathering storm. The rumble of the earthquake rose like tympani, then was split by a shuddering crack that began in the top of the great dome of clouds before crackling down its swirling sides, sharp-edged, ragged, and violent.

The first thundering bolt drove itself down upon the land soon after. Brighter by a thousand times than the faltering moon, the bolt flashed, danced, and flashed again. With a sound that could only be made by a heavenly hammer striking a tremendous anvil, it was then joined by a dozen, a score, and then a hundred more, each striking the top of Mount Solitaire, and dancing atop the great yellow stone altar.

The ground around Michael's body began to smoke, and the smoke rose and swirled around the body to form a cord, and then a column. He tried to move his hands, feel his toes, but still he felt as stiff as a corpse, could barely feel anything beyond the dull, thudding pain in his chest. In the smoky column, a form rose from his own body, looking much like a human form but shrouded as though cocooned. A face came forth, then hands crossed over the chest. As the legs appeared, the arms of the spectral form swept open the column of smoke like a robe and the apparition stepped forward to stand on the mountaintop beside the shattered corpse. There was only one thing missing from the spectral man. In his chest, exactly where his heart should have been, Michael saw only a gaping hole.

The thunder fell off to a distant rumble, the final sigh of a storm giant retiring to bed. In the hush that descended, a gentle pattering of rain began to fall. The peaceful shower further darkened the scorched mountaintop and flushed away the last wisps of smoke. It washed the blood from Michael's face, from the tattered edges of his chest, and it washed the smoke-like cocoon from the face of the one who had stepped forth. Michael opened his mouth and drank the droplets, realizing only in that moment how parched he had become, how ruined by the desert winds.

The water flowed down the chest and arms of the smoke-born man, soaking him from head to toe. The man took a long slow breath and sighed with a mournful smile. He looked down at Michael lying on the blood-stained earth, then knelt and gazed at the body drying in the morning sun. He reached down and gently touched the place on Michael's chest where there had been, until only recently, a gaping wound. The place from which Michael's heart had been so savagely ripped.

"I'm sorry, my friend," the man said, passing his hand over Michael's chest.

Michael stared up at him. He couldn't place the man's face, but he looked so familiar, like a childhood friend found again decades later. The man from the smoke had bright green eyes which peered with compassion down at Michael. His hair was dark with streaks of smoky gray like brushed silver gleaming through it. He had a crooked smile and dimples, which showed despite the gravity of the situation. Michael tried to take a deep breath, feeling like he was going to fall asleep or really die, only he wasn't sure which.

"This is my fault," the man's soft voice said. "I should have been able to stop him. I should have fought harder. But we'll set this right, my friend, we'll bring an end to Lord Striker and return what was stolen to its rightful place."

"Spirit Man," Michael said. His voice was raspy and weak. It was always so strange to see Spirit Man face to face. It was like looking into his own soul, somehow existing outside his body.

"My friend, Michael Seymour, we have walked together through many worlds. I've known you for many years now, perhaps many more than you've known me. Or perhaps you met me long ago and I am only new to the world. Time is a strange thing, my friend. Never as straightforward as we might like it to be.

"You have helped me to do my work across many worlds. I cannot recall all of them, not always. Sometimes they seem a great sweep, pieces and fragments of the same world, and sometimes they are like broken glass that cannot be repaired. But you and I, we have walked over those shards and across those boundaries, and the spirit worlds are better for it.

"I owe you a debt, Michael Seymour. One which might never be repaid. But this is how I shall try. We will recover your heart and bring it back to you. We will banish Lord Striker back to his own world and leave him there. This is what I must do for you, and it is what you must do for me. The stone in your chest is no replacement for a heart. It will only grow heavier as time passes. But you must be strong. You must persevere even as the cold, hard thing in your chest becomes an unbearable burden. You will not have to walk this path alone. I will help you."

Spirit Man bowed his head and closed his eyes for a moment.

"Such a waste of magic and blood, that terrible Lord." His voice held both contempt and awe. "But he has begun his game, and so for now we must play by his rules. I swear to you, Michael Seymour, Spirit of Man, World Walker, that we will hunt down Lord Striker like the animal he is and cut him down."

His head came up and his eyes snapped open, as though he had heard the step of an approaching attacker. Quickly he looked from side to side, tensing himself as though to fight or flee.

"Something on the wind," Spirit Man murmured.

Then he was gone. Michael was once again alone atop the stone altar. Or, not exactly alone, for he felt Spirit Man's presence within him, bolstering him. He still felt the heavy weight of the stone in his chest, the way it clinked against his ribcage. But he could wiggle his fingers, could bend his knees, and finally, at long last, he could stand.

He clucked his tongue and looked around carefully. He flexed his hands and inspected himself. His chest was healed completely, no scars to show that anything had happened at all. He laid his hand over his heart. Nothing. No heartbeat, no sound, no feeling at all. He took his pulse, and again, nothing. If he didn't know better, he would think that he was a statue, a walking corpse. Well. Maybe he was. If he could walk and move, what did it matter if he had no heart? He didn't need a heart to find and kill Lord Striker.

No, not kill. Defeat. He wasn't a killer, was he? Somehow, he couldn't quite remember.

"Well, where do we start?" he said aloud, to no one. "Never a straight line in the other worlds."

He turned around and wasn't terribly surprised to find a magical door waiting for him. The door was blue as the New Mexico sky, and it had a blazing yellow sun painted onto its upper left corner. He walked over to the blue door and stood in front of it and there he saw that it was not really a door at all, but instead a patch of crystal-clear blue sky. And the fiery sun was not painted on at all, but was real and as bright as the sun in his own world. A thin layer of white clouds swirled around and around the sun like a halo. The door did not touch the ground at all, but seemed suspended in midair several feet above the rock platform. Many years ago, all of this might have startled or unnerved him. But Michael had traveled far and wide, had crossed through many such doors, and faced countless wonders and horrors therein. The only difference was that this time, he knew precisely who his enemy was.

Spirit Man watched the clouds within the blue door slowly drift across the deep blue sky. He took a deep breath, braced himself for everything that might await him in the sprawling chaos of the dream world of Shook, and stepped through the door.

Chapter 4

The next thing Michael knew, he was falling. The door had opened not onto any spit of land but into the vastness of open sky. He tried to scream but the air tore the sound from his throat and left him gasping. He struggled for a moment, trying to sort out his sense of up and down, then spread his arms to stabilize his fall as the wind roared past him. Below him stretched the yellows and browns and reds of deserts as far as he could see. He was falling toward a deck of clouds drifting above that landscape. From above him, he heard a sound that was already becoming too familiar with him: the deep rumble of Lord Striker's amused laughter.

"Off to a good start, Spirit Man. Keep your wits about you." His laugh boomed like thunder and then vanished as Michael tumbled away from it.

Michael fell into the clouds and when the white mists surrounded him, he lost all sense of which way he was falling. The winds in the cloud battered him from all directions, knocking him head over heels and tossing him around until he was so dizzy, he could barely see a thing. He was lost to the gray, to the all-encompassing cold. His face went numb as the frigid moisture whipped across his skin. He'd never thought clouds could be so cold. Every second he expected to break out and see the ground below, but the clouds just grew thicker and darker and colder.

Then, just when he thought the sky would black out completely, he broke through the cloud cover and found himself hurtling not toward a desert but toward a broad green sea sparkling in the sun. With a muffled cry of surprise, he flipped himself around to see there was not a cloud in the sky. He could not tell if the sea below was a few hundred feet beneath him, or a few thousand. It was so immense, it may as well have been the entire world. The sound of the wind rushing past him rose in pitch as he fell faster and faster. It rose to a whistle, and then to a scream. His ears popped painfully as the pressure changed. He pulled his hands in to cover his ears, trying to cry out against the wind, against the stabbing pain in his eardrums, but he couldn't hear anything except the high shrieking of the wind.

As he plummeted further, something below him caught his attention. At first it looked like a bit of flotsam adrift in the jade-green sea, and then like a great jagged rock sticking up out of the water. Then, at last, he could identify the shape as a rocky island far below. How high had he been dropped from? How was it even possible for a world to have this much sky? As he fell toward the island faster and faster, his trajectory began to swing toward it until he was flying not downward, but forward, flat above the surface of the sea, rushing toward the island at what must have been hundreds of miles per hour. He couldn't tell if the world had tilted sideways or if some other force besides gravity had begun to act upon him, but he also knew not to ask too many questions when in Shook. It was exhilarating, really, to fly at such an incredible velocity— even if he wasn't exactly controlling the movement. He stretched out his arms and tested a few slight movements, seeing if he could alter his course at all. It was clumsy and mostly ineffective, but it made him feel like Superman—or maybe just Peter Pan, considering how badly he had lost his last fight. Regardless, he hooted with glee as he soared over the sea.

"I'm flying!" he shouted. "I'm flying!"

His joy quickly turned to stomach-churning dread, however, when he realized that, although he was no longer hurtling toward the sea, he was now flying directly toward the island's huge jagged cliffs. The obsidian bluffs stretched for a mile or more to either side, rendering any attempt at steering away almost certainly pointless. Still, he tried to pitch away as best he could, succeeding only in sending himself tumbling out of control for a while until he at last managed to right himself.

Then something collided with him and sent him tumbling again.

When he gathered himself once more, he was astonished to see he was no longer falling, exactly, but riding the front of a huge wave, a rolling ridge of jade ocean a hundred feet high. Sticking out of the gleaming swell of water were the dorsal fins of hundreds of dolphins, cavorting and slaloming along beside him as he rushed directly toward the high black cliff. As the wall filled his view and the rushing of the wave toward it filled his nostrils with the smell of salt, he struggled to keep his head, to keep from trying to scream and filling his lungs with water. The cliff gleamed in the light, the black of the obsidian so polished he could almost see his own reflection in it as he barreled toward certain doom. There was no way around it. All he could do was brace himself as the wave drove him at full speed directly against the sparkling obsidian cliff.

At first he felt that he was still falling, but there was no longer any rush of wind past him. In fact, quite the opposite. Whatever space he now found himself in was completely dark and completely silent. After a few moments, his body adjusted to the stillness and the spinning, dizzying, whirling sensation of motion settled to nothing. He knew he was still plummeting, but with nothing around him in any direction and no air whipping past, it was almost as if he had come to a complete stop. He tried to yell, but the sound did not travel anywhere at all. It did not echo or fade after it left his lips but simply ceased to exist. He could hear himself, but the sound was just sucked up by the darkness as soon as it was produced.

Then he sensed something that made him gasp with a new fear just as great as that of falling—perhaps even more so. In the total darkness, with nothing at all to ground him, Michael smelled something rotting. The overpoweringly sweet stench of Death itself wafted over him and he was reminded of the time when he was a little boy and found a dead mule deer in the desert. For reasons beyond his ability to explain, his first thought was that that same deer must be in this pitch-black space with him now, somehow revived and killed again for his benefit.

Even greater than the scent of death was the feeling of death, the

HEART OF THE SPIRIT MAN

sense that something (or more than one something) had died here, and very recently. From somewhere, a warm, stale breeze emerged. It carried with it that same smell, and as the moist air washed over him, the stench of decomposing matter grew and grew. He tried hard to imagine that the wind could be coming from anywhere, perhaps a crack in the wall of wherever it was he now found himself. But he knew the truth. It was breath.

As if to confirm his fears, before him appeared two huge glowing white eyes. In the light from the eyes, he saw huge jaws, scales flecked with gobbets of rotting flesh, a long sinuous neck ringed with bony plates. Michael choked on thick smoke pouring from the monster's jaws. With all his might, he tried to pull himself away, tried to redirect his hurtling through the void to escape the beast and continue rocketing into the darkness.

"It's just me," the great reptile said in a raspy voice, like dragging a whetstone across a blade. "People call me the Sultan of Shook. I can help you, Spirit Man."

The creature drew nearer, nostrils flaring. The smell of death became so overpowering, Michael almost vomited as he tumbled through the air. At this rate he would never outpace the creature, which moved so effortlessly through the air, as if it were nothing. He had to think fast.

"How can you help me?" he said. Though the dark stole the words as soon as he spoke them, the creature seemed to hear, and its teeth came together in a wicked smile.

"I can show you the way. You have such a long journey ahead of you, Spirit Man, let me take you where you need to go." It came even closer, just a few feet away now. "Poor little thing, so out of place in this realm. Can't even fly properly. Come to me and I will take care of everything for you."

Michael twisted in the air and allowed himself to drift closer to the beast. Closer...closer...until he was nearly touching the thing's foul snout. He had to hold his breath as great waves of decay washed over him, emanating from deep within the Sultan's gut. Surely only death awaited him there.

"That's it, little one," the Sultan said. "Just a little closer."

Just as he was about to make contact, Michael abruptly pivoted in the air and slammed one of his feet as hard as he could into the creature's glowing eye. It shrieked and clawed at him just as he dodged out of its reach. He watched it go tumbling away into the dark, clutching at its wounded eye and bellowing all the way.

And again Michael heard the rumbling voice and derisive laughter of Lord Striker.

"I guess he just doesn't like dragons, Sultan."

And the Sultan's voice called out after him too, saying, "No way out of this nightmare, Spirit Man, no way out at all! Darkness ahead for you, my friend!" A breathy, smoky laugh followed him and slowly died down as he flew past.

Not knowing if he had passed an obstacle or failed a test, Michael floated into the black. Where had he gone wrong? He had been dumped into terrible worlds before, places of horrible violence, but he couldn't remember feeling so helpless for a long time, like he had no control over where he was going. The last time he recalled feeling this way had been on his very first journey into Shook, when the dread soldiers of Gehenna had set upon him and dragged him to their dungeon. He was older now, wiser. How had Lord Striker gotten the better of him so easily? If he could only find a way to stop and get his bearings, maybe he could start trying to formulate an actual plan, find something to grab onto, anything but more of this horrible darkness.

He lost track of how long he hurtled through the pitch black, but it felt like it had been hours before his eye detected a tiny speck of light which seemed at first incredibly small but which he soon realized was just very far away. What happened next occurred so fast, he did not even have time to react. The speck rapidly grew to a spot, a circle, and then a flashing disc as it rushed toward him. He threw up his arms to shield himself, but the disc flashed right past him, leaving him hanging in space in light so bright he couldn't see a thing at first. Spots of different colors danced across his vision, blinking in and out of existence as he squinted and tried to adjust to the sudden glare. After all that darkness, he felt practically blinded by the light.

"What the hell is going on?" he shouted, more to himself than to anyone who might answer. But then something peculiar happened: The light around him pulsed, then dimmed until it was no longer painful to look at. Michael blinked away tears from the sting of the brightness.

Then, finally, after that eternity of flight or falling or whatever the hell it had been, Michael landed on solid ground. He struck, twisted, tumbled backward in a clumsy roll, and came to rest lying on his face. Quickly, he ran his hands over his body, feeling for any injuries. Somehow, nothing was broken. He had a few aches, but none more significant than he might have acquired after falling from a stepladder. Perhaps, at some point during his long descent, his fall had slowed without his realizing it. He was hungry and his ears still stung from the screaming winds of his descent, but otherwise he felt completely intact.

He found himself grinning from ear to ear. It felt better than he would have believed to finally have his feet on solid ground again. He'd never understood, before, how shipwrecked sailors could kiss the sand when they finally made it ashore after days at sea, but he was feeling a pretty strong impulse to get puckering on the gray stone beneath him right about now.

He lay on the ground for a few moments, trying to gauge his surroundings without looking. If whatever had stopped him was something malevolent, it would be better for him if they thought he was unconscious and unaware. He could get the drop on them that way. But after a minute or two, nothing attacked him, and so he slowly lifted his head, using his elbows to brace himself as he gradually shifted into a sitting position and dusted himself off. He bowed his head and took a deep breath.

"All right, Michael," he murmured to himself. "You're alive. That's step one. You've been in worse scrapes before. That was basically just hardcore skydiving. You're going to stand up, and we're going to figure out what's going on and why we're here, and you'll get out of this alive, just like everything else you've gotten out of alive." It felt strange, talking to himself, but he needed to hear a real voice after so long in that bizarre space between spaces.

He took another deep, bracing breath and looked up. And he immediately gave a cry of dismay.

Before him rose the great yellow stone, looking almost exactly like it had the last time he saw it, when Lord Striker tore out his beating heart. Across its rugged face were splashed words, in thickening blood: "SHOOK: TO HELL AND BACK AGAIN."

Back on Solitaire! But how? He had traveled so far. He staggered over to the stone and tilted his head. There was something different this time, though he couldn't put his finger on it. It was as if he was looking at two images and trying to spot the difference, only here, it wasn't something visual. It was more like some sixth sense was tugging at his sleeve, insisting that something had changed in the very air, in the smell, in the molecular makeup of the world around him. Even the trees surrounding the clearing made him oddly uneasy, moved in a way that set his hairs on edge. The dirt underfoot, too, was off. He scooped up a clump of it and let it run through his fingers and something about the weight of it, the texture, just wasn't right. No, this place might look an awful lot like where he'd been atop Mount Solitaire, but there was no doubt in his mind that it was, in fact, somewhere else entirely.

He didn't like it. Not one bit. If Lord Striker had been telling the truth—if he really was the Lord of Shook—then he could bend this world and its rules however he saw fit. Lord Striker could create, destroy, remake it all in whatever way suited him.

Michael peered through the dense forest and ran a hand through his tousled hair. He was in far deeper trouble than he had first thought.

Chapter 5

Michael sat down heavily in the brown and yellow dust of the mountaintop and shook his head at the bloody letters splattered on the stone above him. To hell and back again? No, he wasn't back from hell. Not at all. If anything, he was only going deeper into it. Even so, he looked in the direction of the path he had first taken to get to the clearing and the great yellow stone, hoping against hope that it might be possible to just walk back down the path and return to the waking world, where everything he had experienced would prove itself to be nothing more than a bad dream, perhaps the product of an overnight storm. But he knew, even as he hoped, that it would not be. As he stood, the stone knocked about in his chest, a constant reminder of what he had lost. He touched the spot again where there ought to have been a scar and found, to his surprise, that it was no longer completely unblemished. There, directly over his heart, was a speck of discoloration. He ran his fingers over it and it felt hard and cold, not a part of his flesh but somehow connected to it inextricably. Whatever it was, it couldn't be good news. His stomach curled in on itself. In any case, it was a problem for another time. Right now, he had more pressing concerns. First off, wasn't it about time he found some proper clothes? This torn janitor's jumpsuit was starting to get old.

Michael walked to the edge of the clearing, peering down through the trees in the direction which ought to have revealed the glittering sprawl of Las Cruces. But when he looked out beyond the clearing, all he could see were trees, the wild forest tumbling for miles and miles before him, and all he could hear was wind in the trees. Only as he looked closer did he realize why everything looked so different now. The sun had risen. It floated high in the sky, beating down with all its might. But why hadn't he felt it earlier? He extended his hand to catch the sun's rays and found them diminished somehow. It wasn't that he didn't feel the warmth at all—because he did—but rather that it was muted, less than it ought to have been. And for that matter the smell of pine, too, had grown fainter since his first trek up to this mountaintop. The world felt as if it was receding from him, a tide going out with no promise that it would return. Was this what it meant to have no heart? Was he already, so quickly, forgetting what it meant to be whole?

Just then, he heard a strange sound begin to rise around him, and whipped around to see what was causing it, half expecting another assault by Lord Striker. The sound started as a low hum but soon swelled to a tremendous roar, like a tornado tearing across the countryside. It seemed to be coming from behind the great stone pillar. As Michael watched, a cloud of yellow dust rose up from behind the stone, swirling slowly at first, then faster and faster, around and around, until it became an impossibly huge dust devil, churning there in the clearing. Instinctively, Michael hit the deck, sprawling on his belly to make himself less obvious, keeping his eyes on the dust devil.

The tornado continued rising and then, once it hovered over the trees themselves, did something Michael was sure tornadoes weren't supposed to do. It extended its narrow base and began to run it, finger-like, across the trees. The probing tip of that swirling mass of dust and violence poked here and there as though looking for something. Or someone.

Michael began to crawl into the denser part of the forest to escape that windy tentacle, trying with all his might not to break any twigs along the way. As he crawled, the aches and pains from his fall flared up all at once and it was all he could do not to groan and give away his location. The whirling cloud of yellow dust swept here and there overhead, its twitching finger probing and searching, its great bulk blotting out the sun and casting a sinister shadow over Michael's cowering body.

As the dust devil stroked the tops of the tall trees crowning the mountain, they quavered and whipped back and forth like blades of grass beneath the whirling blades of a lawnmower, no longer regal and stoic, but now just fragile stalks caught in a terrible storm. The dust swirled everywhere, coating Michael's skin in a layer of debris. He covered his eyes to keep the dust out, and kept his mouth clamped shut. Even still, his tongue slid against grit on his teeth. Keeping his eyes covered, he tried to pick out any safe haven from the dust, any shelter he could move to, anywhere he'd be safer than where he was now, hiding beneath the trembling shadow of the forest. A clattering sound drew his eye and he saw that pebbles of bigger and bigger sizes were lifting into the air, drawn into the dust devil's whirling winds. Larger rocks followed the smaller rocks, until the gale was filled with deadly projectiles whipping around at positively lethal speeds. If he ended up on the wrong side of one of those, Michael knew he'd be finished.

After a few moments of its unsuccessful search, the dust devil appeared to become frustrated. Rather than probing through the trees, it instead began to rip them from the earth, roots and all. One after another, and then many at once, it tore the trees from the mountain and hauled their huge trunks into its mass like they weighed nothing at all. Branches snapped, pine needles were stripped away, and the howling dust storm became a churning chaos of dark greens and browns as if some druidic beast, a long-forgotten god of the woods, had awoken.

Michael grabbed hold of a particularly hardy root which had re-mained planted in the ground as its trunk snapped away and fell into the sky. He wrapped both his arms around it and held on for dear life as the gale lifted him bodily from the dirt and pulled him sky-ward. For a moment they battled that way, the dust devil pulling and Michael refusing to release the root. Then, finally, the pull ceased and Michael fell back to the ground with a painful thump.

Frantic, he looked out across the utterly transformed landscape in search of any way out. But there was nowhere left to run. Every last tree had been torn from the mountaintop and now swirled and shattered and spun in the madness of the gale overhead. All that remained was broken earth and jagged rock and, of course, the stone altar looming over it all.

Michael expected, then, that the dust devil would reach its wicked finger down to him and wrench him free of his handhold. But instead, the whole mass simply settled into place directly above him. Then, the side of the swirling mass began to flex up, as though the winds were flowing over an inverted glass dome. At last, it split open entirely, and Michael saw a tall and imposing figure standing in the midst of the storm. Who else but Lord Striker again? Resplendent in his blue robe, his gold mask, perfect golden locks falling across his shoulders. Like the Colossus, he stood with feet apart and hands on hips, and the ringing, rumbling of his laughter echoed from the storm, louder even than the howling of the spinning tornado.

"Still here, Spirit Man?" Lord Striker called over the howling wind. "I must say, I expected more from you! Why, you haven't moved an inch. I thought you were going to hunt me down, make a hero of yourself and an example out of me? What's the matter? Is your heart not in it?"

He held up the crystal decanter with the silver binding on its stopper, and Michael could clearly see the bloody heart inside. He stumbled backward until he crashed hard against the altar. He held one arm across his face to shield himself from the whipping wisps of the edges of the storm, but with the other hand, he reached for something, anything, he could use as a weapon.

The blue-robed demigod from Shook began to shake the jar back and forth and the heart slapped against one side and then the other, thu-thunk, thu-thunk, thu-thunk, louder and louder. Oh, how Michael yearned to feel those impacts. They would be painful, to be sure, but to see his heart battered about like that and feel nothing was somehow far worse. It felt like the symptom of some terrible, incurable disease.

His hand closed around a rock the size of his fist. Heavy and solid. It might not hurt Lord Striker much, but if he could only hit the decanter....

"Okay, Striker," he shouted. Slowly, he slid the rock to his side. "You win. Clearly, I'm no match for your power." He edged forward a little. Almost in range now. "Now how about we call it quits, huh?"

Lord Striker laughed. Michael was starting to get awfully sick of that damn laugh.

"That is the old saying, isn't it," said Lord Striker. "Quit while you're ahead? But, you know, I've never been one to play by someone else's rules. I've always walked to the beat of...my own drum." He held the beating heart up to his ear and grinned.

This was the chance Michael was waiting for. In one clean motion, he raised the rock and pelted it directly at the crystal in Lord Striker's hands. The hunk of stone sailed through the air fast and true. To Michael, it moved almost in slow motion as it arced directly toward its target. He couldn't believe it. It would be a perfect hit!

But then, just as the rock should have struck the jar, it passed straight through instead. There was no shattering of glass, no falling heart. It was as if Michael had thrown a rock at smoke.

"Oh, come now, Michael," Lord Striker said with a chuckle. "You didn't think I was really here, did you?" His form wavered, becoming suddenly immaterial along with the decanter and the heart inside. "Unlike you, I've got lots I must be doing. I can't spend all day hanging around this mountaintop. Big things await, Spirit Man. Big things."

With that, the mass of dust swirled around Lord Striker again, obscuring him from view. The storm rose straight up into the air like an enormous spaceship, darkening the sun at first, then disappearing right into it.

"Damn you!" Michael yelled, raising his fist to the sky. "What are you afraid of? Come back here, you big ugly blue chicken! Come back here and face me!" It was an absurd challenge, of course. He'd been so badly beaten last time that he had very little hope of winning any kind of head-to-head fight. But he didn't know what else to do. He was in Lord Striker's world, playing by Lord Striker's rules. How could he ever hope to catch him and recover his heart? Well, he'd have to figure something out, and soon. He didn't even want to imagine what Lord Striker's plans might be with the organ.

He leaned back against the altar and lightly knocked his head against it several times in frustration.

"Where to next?" he said.

As if in answer, a dark spot crossed directly overhead, momentarily disappearing in the blinding rays of the sun but then reappearing once more in the blue sky beyond. A bird of some kind? Michael realized he hadn't seen another bird since beginning this journey. It had to mean something, didn't it? He followed the creature with his eyes as it swooped lower and soared toward the horizon.

Feeling very unsatisfied with his own performance and eager for something to change, Michael shook himself off and set out after the bird. It was slow going, for the most part. The land where the trees had been uprooted was utterly ruined, shattered, a mess of overturned earth and fragments of rock. Michael had to pick his way through at a painfully slow pace to keep from tripping. To make matters worse, the ground was a steep slope, and all it would take would be one wrong step to send him careening down and down and down the hill. He'd had quite enough of falling for one day, thank you very much.

After a while, he found himself stepping out onto a broad ridge overlooking the valley below. And what a valley it was! It was certainly not the Mesilla Valley of New Mexico from which he had come. As beautiful as that valley was, the one which unfurled before him now absolutely put it to shame.

A path began where he stood and wound through softly-rolling hills and over gentle streams. The ground was a magic carpet full of wild flowers and tall grasses bending and waving in the playful breeze. A little ways off, the flowered carpet met another forest and gave way to a grove of gorgeous aspens. It was into this grove the bird flew, so Michael followed.

Shaking off his aches and the sense of helplessness that had alighted on his shoulders, he strode quickly down the trail. After a moment he began to jog, and finally to run. He felt the adrenaline rise in his body, the power driving his legs forward with astonishing speed. But something crucial was missing. He ran faster and faster, waiting for the joy of it to wash over him as it always had...but that joy never came. He ran not like a man but like a machine, sprinting without passion, without the hot flow of blood in his veins, driven forward only by a cold clarity of purpose. Gravity ushered him down the hillside even faster and the wind whipped past his ears and still nothing changed. He was struck by a memory of running down a hill like this years ago with his friend Mark, hooting and laughing the whole way. It felt like a different life, a different person entirely. The stone sat cold and lifeless in his chest, refusing him even this small bit of love, the love of movement. It did not beat in time with his pumping legs, did not beat at all.

But there was no time to get lost in such disappointments. The aspens awaited him and he pushed himself harder and harder to reach them as the bird vanished beneath their shadow. He ran not like an antelope, but like the streaking cheetah that chases the antelope, shuddering in anticipation of the taste of blood. He didn't so much as slow as he crossed from the meadow into the grove, suddenly drenched in shadow as he ran. Michael was barely skimming the ground, as though just flying above it and reaching down with his feet to spring off the ground to drive himself, hurtling forward ever faster. He searched the branches overhead for the bird as he ran, barely paying attention to the path ahead. Then, *bam!* A thick branch struck him squarely across the forehead, sending him somersaulting backwards through the air as his body continued forward, so he landed flat on his face in the middle of the trail. He hit his heard hard on a rock and blacked out.

Michael had no idea how long he lay there. It might have been seconds or hours or even days. As he began to come back to his senses, he felt his breathing grow calm and slow. The ringing pain in his head gradually subsided. He raised his head and was surprised to find a sculpture had been erected exactly in the middle of the trail. It depicted a tall and gaunt man in tattered black clothes and the top hat of an old-fashioned undertaker, who held a wide signboard in his hands. It read: "KNOCK YOURSELF OUT AND FIND YOURSELF IN A NEW WORLD." The teeth of the statue gleamed bright white, made of brighter marble than the rough gray stone of the rest of the sculpture. Had that been what knocked him down?

Michael groaned and lay back down, hoping his throbbing head-ache would recede if he only gave it a moment. At least Lord Striker was nowhere to be seen. Then again, neither was the bird who had led Michael here. As his eyes adjusted to the dusky grove, Michael saw that the trail had led him to the shores of a small, shallow pond. The pretty pool was surrounded by lush greenery and dark-colored blossoms that seemed carved from translucent wax. In the man-ner of a Japanese garden, a lovely bridge stretched over the water. *Well, that must be something,* he thought. He hauled himself up and stumbled over to the bridge. When he stepped onto it, a cloud of white snow geese rose up together from the lake and flapped off into the sky. He gasped in awe at the sight. Those thousands of wings all beating together created a thrilling sound like a distant rainstorm as the geese flew up over the top of the canopy. He stood clutching the ivory railing of the bridge (no longer white but stained coffee-brown as though from centuries of human contact). High above, the cloud of geese shaped itself into a long "V" which turned round and round above the lake, and then finally disappeared into the distance. The V seemed to point in the same direction as he had been running, which must have been a good sign. If he couldn't trust the birds of this strange land, who could he trust?

Michael leaned over the railing and looked down into the clear water. He smiled at the tall slender green reeds and light brown cat-tails which grew at the base of the bridge pylons. A school of spotted red koi and white carp swam in intricate, indecipherable patterns at the bottom of the shallow lake. He could get used to this sort of place. Best not to be lulled into a false sense of security, though. For all he knew, any of these very fish could transform into the hulking Lord Striker at any second. Still, it was hard to see evil in such a beautiful environment, and for a moment he allowed himself to fall back into a nostalgic reverie. This beautiful place, surrounded, he now saw, by snow-dusted mountains in the far distance, reminded Spirit Man very much of the Bosque Del Apache Bird Sanctuary in

New Mexico. The memory of that sanctuary was a pleasant one, but its distance from him turned it sad as well. Homesick, lost, and lonely, Michael closed his eyes. He wanted to go home, to return to his old life. But would it even be the same with a heart made of stone? Would the bird sanctuary stoke in him the same awe and joy it had before, or would he find himself staring blankly, unable to feel a single thing? Once more, he touched the place on his chest from whence Lord Striker had torn out his heart and was startled to find that the discolored patch had grown to about the size of a quarter. He ran his finger across its surface and found it rough and hard to the touch. Was that...could it be...stone?

Before he could investigate any further, he heard a voice from behind him, squeaky and strangely familiar.

"To err is human; to err a whole bunch, divine," said the voice.

Michael spun around on his heels, fists up, ready to face his enemy, and was surprised at what he saw.

At the end of the bridge stood a man as strange-looking as anyone he had ever met. He was not four feet tall, with almost comically stumpy legs. His hips and his butt were wide and round, as though a clay model of a normal man had been squashed down to spread out into this short, girthy specimen Michael now saw before him. His shoulders were broad, though not especially large, but short arms were gnarled with muscles. Most astonishing was his head, which was tall and round like a melon, with a high forehead and a face all squinched down close to a wide but very short chin.

"Hey, Spirit Man! Glad to see you made it here to these tricks of the sticks!" He gave a jolly laugh.

"Do I know you?" Michael asked. He tried to keep himself from looking too surprised at the man's unusual appearance. From the very top of the little man's head sprouted a woolly bristle of curly black hair, and from the very bottom of his wide jaw sprouted a scraggle of long red beard which extended all the way to his pot belly. He was wearing a pair of dark purple tights, a pair of dirty white tennis shoes, and a bright yellow sweatshirt stained with spaghetti sauce and chocolate pudding. He walked—or, more accurately, bounced—on his stubby bowlegs over to Michael and put out his stubby-fingered hand to shake.

"In a manner of speaking," he said in his high, wheezy voice. "I am Lazaro Hitchcock, and I am the wizard in this crack of the track here in mother-shaking Shook! Pleased to meet you, Spirit Man! Heard so much about you! All good of course!"

Michael cautiously put out his own hand, and Lazaro shook his hand vigorously for a much longer time than he was frankly comfortable with. When they had shaken hands so long it began to seem ridiculous, Michael broke out in a big grin. Hadn't he just been feeling terribly lonely? And here was this funny little man who seemed all too eager to be his friend.

Lazaro finally released his grip, let out a whoop of laughter, and leapt right up into the air with surprising grace. He performed a clumsy but earnest back flip and landed right on his butt before bouncing back up to his feet.

Michael laughed in genuine delight.

"Well, Lazaro Hitchcock," he said, "I am very pleased to meet you. That is, as long as you're not in league with Lord Striker."

"Not a chance, Mister Strange-pants!" Lazaro then leaned in and whispered, "Can't stand the fellow myself, but don't tell anyone or I could be in big trouble."

The diminutive wizard then jumped up and down, spun around in midair, and popped right over in a back flip again. Once again, he didn't quite stick the landing, crashed onto his backside, and bounded to his feet apparently unscathed.

"You're a big fella, ain't ya?" Lazaro said. "Yes, you are! Wow! They make them real big where you come from. Come on now, Spirit Man, follow me! You got to get the scoop on all the goop around here! That's an expression 'round these parts meaning we got a lot to talk about! So let's go, Spirit Man! What say we go chew a shoe?"

Michael blinked in confusion, trying to parse all the strange things the wizard was throwing at him. He looked back toward the beautiful lake with longing.

"Where are we going?" He didn't want to leave this first slice of peace he'd found since he'd landed in Shook. But he also had a feeling there wouldn't be much choice in the matter.

"To go eat! What else? Isn't your tummy tum hungry? Plenty of grub at my humble hut!" Lazaro gave a great belly laugh, scampered down the bridge, and began to bound along the trail. He sure managed a lot of height for such a small guy.

Michael sighed, took one parting look at the water, then followed Lazaro. Going with the flow, however bizarre, was often the only acceptable course of action in the worlds he had traveled. Lazaro appeared trustworthy, at least for now, so maybe he could help Michael track down Lord Striker and his heart. And if the wizard ended up being not so trustworthy after all...well, Michael would cross that bridge when he came to it.

Chapter 6

Though Michael was a tall man with long legs—not to mention a champion runner as well—and Lazaro was a short man with stumpy legs, Michael found it difficult to keep up with the enthusiastic wizard. The red-bearded man bounded along like a bouncing ball, his little legs pumping madly back and forth. As the narrow dirt path led through the thick woods, passing tall, skinny trees and flowers in the undergrowth, the little cheerful guy was always a step or two in front of Spirit Man. They ran for hours through the woods with the warm sunlight filtering through the trees and dancing upon their faces and shoulders. Tall poplar trees grew in this part of the woods and their golden leaves rustled against one another in the gentle wind, filling Michael's ears with sweet sounds. Michael kept expecting Lazaro to tire or ask for a break (even at an easy jog, Michael was starting to get tired) but they kept on at a steady pace, weaving their way through the forest.

Eventually, they came to a small clearing and Lazaro held up a meaty hand to signal that they should stop at the edge of it. There in the middle of the small clearing stood a magnificent brown stone castle. It towered over the trees and looked like something straight out of a storybook, with tall spires and battlements and banners. The flags billowing from the tallest towers had a cartoonish version of Lazaro's face on them, winking and grinning widely.

"Welcome," said Lazaro, "to my simple home."

"Wow. That is some humble hut!" Michael said, laughing. To tell the truth, he had been expecting something barely a step above a cave—perhaps some moss-covered dwelling carved out of a hillside, redolent with damp leaves and mildew. But this? There was something so secure about it, so warm and welcoming, that for the first time since his arrival in Shook, Spirit Man felt completely safe and far from danger. He tried to imagine Lord Striker showing up here and it was impossible to picture his great blue-robed tormentor even in the same space as this comfortable castle.

"I call this place The Little Dakota," Lazaro said. "Hope you like it, Spirit Man. Hope, hope, hope you like it. I do."

"It's beautiful, Lazaro. Does anyone else live here?"

"Oh, gosh no. Just little old me. Nobody else can bother me that way, if you know what I mean. Like it like that. Keep to my little old self, just a little old elf! Come on, let's go. We don't got all day and I could eat a whole shuffle of buffalo if they had them out here on the range."

Michael shook his head with a chuckle at the little wizard's strange manner of speech and followed without another word. He was hungry too. Starving, really. He couldn't even remember how long it had been since he had last eaten.

They walked on a wide pathway made of blood-red pipestone carved with thousands of fish, lizards, and tiny men with big lemur eyes and long tails. Waiting to greet them were twin towers emerging from the castle's roof of thick tar and old worn gray shingles. Though the castle was enormous, it had been constructed with the proportions of Lazaro's body in mind. There was a short, wide archway leading through the front gates, and Michael had to duck his head and crouch a little to avoid bumping his head as they entered the courtyard.

Michael thought he must have been transported back in time. A white marble fountain in the middle of the courtyard flowed with crystal clear bubbling water. The water splashed down the white marble fountain and the sound of its burbling echoed from wall to wall, becoming a playful sort of sonic dance that moved here and there across the courtyard. The sound washed away all Michael's worries, at least temporarily. Across the courtyard stood a weathered wooden door, just five feet tall. Above it on the wall was a beautiful sign, carved in white marble to match the fountain. It read: "THE WAY TO A MAN'S HEART IS THROUGH HIS STOMACH!"

"I once had a girlfriend who told me that," Michael said. He wasn't sure why Wendy came to mind then. He hadn't thought about her in so long…and hadn't seen her in even longer. "She was a great cook, really, though I'll admit that with my 'help,' we managed to burn more than one soufflé." He thought back to Wendy's smile and the way she looked at him when they cooked together and he couldn't remember the way the food even tasted. He tried to remember what it felt like to hold her and couldn't recall that either. Whatever warmth had once been attached to those memories belonged to him no longer.

"Without appetite, no fulfillment," said Lazaro with a bob of his head and the air of a wise man speaking a great philosophy. "Let's see what you do have an appetite for."

It was such a strange thing to say, all things considered, and Michael wondered how much of his predicament Lazaro knew. Could he see the discolored patch growing across Michael's chest? Did he know what it meant? Questions for another time, perhaps.

Lazaro opened the old wooden door and they went inside the castle itself. It was dim inside, but the torchlight illuminating the space gave it a cozy, fireside feeling.

"Food's awaitin' Spirit Man, but first," Lazaro said, stopping by a door and fiddling with an oversized ring of keys, "we've gotta get you some proper garments. Those old raggedy rags just won't do." He wrenched open the door, revealing a small, crowded room jam-packed with chests which were themselves packed with clothes—so many that none of the chests closed properly.

"I'm sure somethin' in there'll fit ya, Spirit Man. Have a look."

Michael did as he was told and dug around in the jumble for a while. He had expected to find only oddly-sized clothing made for Lazaro's particular build, but found clothing of all shapes and sizes in the assortment of chests. There were motorcycle jackets, geisha robes, cowboy hats bigger than any he had ever seen, baby-sized sweatpants, and much more besides.

"Where on earth did you get all this stuff?" Michael said.

"Not on earth! Why, you wouldn't believe all the crazy style crazes crossin' through every crook and cranny of Shook day in and day

                    HEART OF THE SPIRIT MAN

out. One day it's in, next day it's out! I just gather up what folks leave behind in case I needs it—which, I might point out, I did today!"

In the end, Michael settled on a simple button-up shirt and jeans. He felt pretty out of place in that grand castle, but hey, at least he was comfortable.

Next, they walked down a long hallway and came at last to the dining hall, where the smell of food hung heavy in the air. The hall was vast, and held a dozen round tables in two rows across the center. A long row of big picture windows stretched all the way around three sides of the spacious dining room and dispelled the dim and any need for torches. Beyond those big picture windows flourished Lazaro's splendid flower and herb gardens.

"Sit down wherever ya like, Spirit Man! I'll be right back with the soup of the day!" Lazaro scurried off to the main kitchen through a door in the back of the room. Did he really live here all alone? It was almost sad, in a way—all this space for one unusually small man.

Michael sat down at one of the tables and took his time admiring his surroundings. Every table in the dining hall was neatly covered with a white tablecloth. Atop each of these rested neatly folded green napkins and pure crystal glasses, as well as silverware polished so painstakingly it sparkled in the sunlight. Did Lazaro have servants who set the table for him, or was this room always left this way? Michael held a spoon up to his face and he could see his own reflection in it. Definitely not dusty, like Michael might expect if the room was always set. But why lay out all these places for one guest? For a moment Michael thought perhaps he had walked into a trap and would see Striker's image in the silver spoon, but a second later the feeling passed. With a sigh he put the spoon back down on the table next to his dinner plate, white with blue trim.

Soon Lazaro came skipping out into the dining room, carrying a silver tray with two hot bowls of steaming soup, somehow not spilling a single drop. The fragrant, savory scent of the soup filled up the entire room and swirled round and round in Michael's nostrils. It reminded him of his grandmother's homemade chicken soup which she cooked with fresh vegetables and herbs from her garden.

"Lazaro, that smells delicious."

"Ever heard of Murff Ball Soup?" Lazaro asked with a wink, setting one bowl in front of Michael and another across the table. He pulled his chair out and then bounced over the back of it to land facing Michael with a grin. Was he a wizard or a gymnast?

"No, what is it?" Michael asked, not really sure if he wanted to know. He lifted his spoon and prodded at the soup, which looked like the chicken soup it smelled like. But things were rarely as they seemed in Shook.

"It's your basic chicken soup—little of this, and a little of that. Just with a secret little secret. But don't go askin' because I swore I'd never tell!"

Lazaro picked up his own spoon, smiled at Michael, then leaned over his bowl of Murff Ball soup and took a huge slurping sip. Using a big silver spoon, Michael took a sip from his own bowl—though not as loud or as rude as the wizard's. It was, he had to admit, an incredibly good soup. Lazaro took another slurp, louder than the one before, fully enjoying himself. When he saw Michael's face light up at the delicious taste of his famous Murff Ball soup, he bounced up and down in his chair, giggling.

Michael chuckled as well. "I don't know what's in this soup, but I'd wager it probably makes wizards out of ordinary men." He dipped eagerly into the bowl, bringing out big chunks of tender chicken, mushrooms, and golden squash. No matter how much he ate, the level of soup in the bowl never seemed to go down, and by the time he realized it may very well be bottomless, he had already eaten what must have been three bowls' worth of soup.

"Oh, I forgot," Lazaro said. He reached into the pocket of his baggy pants and brought out a crusty loaf of fresh-baked bread. He tore it in half, gave half to Michael, and dipped his own hunk into the soup. After subtly inspecting the bread (those pants didn't exactly look like they'd been washed recently), Michael did the same. The bread, despite its origin, was every bit as good as the soup—maybe even better. By the time the bread was gone, the bowl had finally allowed itself to run dry, and it couldn't have happened at a better time, because Michael couldn't eat another bite.

The wizard let out a big burp and wiped his mouth off with the sleeve of his bright yellow sweatshirt. He leaned back in his chair and gave a deep, contented sigh.

"Okay, Spirit Man, as you probably figured, we're not just here to slurp soup and bake bread. So here's the real deal, the deal of steel. You want to know about Striker, Lord of Shook, who's been giving you a doozy of a time." His voice was suddenly serious, more serious than it had been since Michael had met the odd little man.

Michael sat up straighter in his chair and nodded gravely. "I do," he said.

He wasn't quite sure how Lazaro knew that this was what Michael wanted to know about, but he wasn't wrong. The more Michael knew about Lord Striker, the better chance he'd have to take him down and get his heart back. And he needed all the advantage he could get.

"I thought as much, as much and such. Well, you're a lucky ducky, Buck, 'cause I'm going to tell you all that I can. There is so much you need to know and so little precious time for me to tell you the whole story, because it is a very long one filled with history dating back to the beginning of time itself. Y'see, Lord Striker belongs to what we out here call the Clan of the Dangerous Gods. I'll spare ya the details, but the short and round of it is that they're the meanest, wickedest, and most violent of all the Pantheon here in Shook. And Lord Striker is the meanest, wickedest, and most violent of all them! He likes to call himself the Lord of Shook, and to tell ya the truth, that's not so spittin' far off from being the reality of this here situation. These days, murder is his business. Sufferin'. Torment. He brings death and destruction upon the land and he shows no remorse for what he has done, and not one man or frog has got the guts to stand up to him. Spirit Man, here in Shook we are born to die, not to live. That's how it is under Lord Striker's rule and reign of terror here in this sad place. Innocent men, women, and children have been felled by his mighty hand, one by one or lots at once, limb by limb or all limbs at once...heart by heart. All we have has been taken away from us.

Everything Lord Striker touches dies, and becomes death itself. No man, woman, or child, no elf or fairy, no demigod or demon, can ever escape The Ultimate Law, which is death by His Hand."

"Is he a god?" Michael said, dreading the answer. He'd never gone up against a god before, at least as far as he knew....He needed more information. It was one thing to fight a man, another entirely to fight a god.

Lazaro got a far-away look in his eye, like he was recalling something he didn't much want to recall.

"Hard to say. What is a god in Shook, anyway? A master of death? Or maybe a slave to it. One thing you'd better believe is that he sure acts like he thinks he is the One True God of All the Universes. But here's the tricky bit, Flick. Question isn't what is he, but what was he."

"I don't understand."

"Lotta ideas kickin' here and there across Shook about where Striker came from and how he got to be so awfully abominable, but here's one I heard that might interest your little ears, little deer." He leaned in close, conspiratorially. "I heard he used to be called hero. Like you and your Spirit Man. I heard he saved our crooked Shook not once or twice but a hundred and a half times. I'm talkin' long, long ago. Before he went mad."

Lazaro coughed—or maybe laughed, it was hard to tell.

"Anywho, Emmylou, I don't know if he is a god or a demon, if he is good or evil, or maybe a little good and a lot of evil, but around these parts of the carts, he carries a very big stick, and it's a very tricky stick, Dick, let me clue you."

"Wait," Michael said. "What do you mean he used to be—"

Lazaro waved him away.

"I said everything I know 'bout all that. Now do ya wanna find the scoundrel or what?"

"I do. Is he close by?"

"Now that's a good question. Lucky for me and unlucky for you, Striker's nowhere near my humble hut. Fact is, he lives on a place called Terminal Island. That's where you'll find The Tower of Views and The Garden of Two Deaths. And that's where you'll find our lovely lad Lord Striker."

"Can you tell me how to get there, Lazaro?"

"Nope, 'fraid not." Lazaro sighed and leaned back in his seat, crossing his hands over his belly. "Nobody has ever seen these secret places and lived to tell about them. Terminal Island, The Tower of Views, and the Garden of Two Deaths are all myth to everyone dying here in Shook. That's the catch of the latch here, y'see what I mean. Spirit Man, until you can see it with your own eyes and feel the ground below your own stinking feet, well, it might just be another illusion."

Michael stared at him, trying to make some sense of what Lazaro was trying to say. If no one even knew if Terminal Island was real, then where was he supposed to go from here? What could he trust to be more than a trick, a trap, or a simple dead end?

"I am very sorry, Spirit Man," said the little man with the wheezing voice and jiggling jowls. "I can't tell you much more about the towers and secret gardens. But I will tell you this much. My gut feeling, which is about the only thing I trust, tells me that the heart Lord Striker has stolen is not lost. My dear friend, he has a purpose for your heart. A most purposeful plan. Only I can't say precisely what that might be."

He leaned back in his chair with a great sigh.

"I have spent many long years guessing what he truly wants," said Lazaro. "From all of us. You know what I've come up with?"

"What?"

Lazaro spread his hands. "Not a clumsy, clunking clue. Not for little old me to know, I think. But for you, maybe. I could see maybe for you."

Michael ran his spoon along the rim of his empty bowl. He had hoped Lazaro might have a solution, perhaps some kind of weapon he could use to fight against Lord Striker. Instead, he had given him only riddles, unanswerable questions, and a creeping dread in his gut.

"There's one other thing," Lazaro said. "You might truly die if you reach the garden." He said it casually, as if it were nothing.

"Excuse me?"

Lazaro shrugged. "Well, there's different ways to die, aren't there? Dying's really just another trip, huh, Skip? But let me tell you something about what dying twice means. The first death is the killing of the body like when someone murders you, strikes you down with a sword or a hammer."

Michael nodded. He certainly knew what it felt like to die. If lying atop that stone altar with his chest split open and his heart beating in Lord Striker's hand hadn't been a lesson in physical death, he didn't know what was.

"The second death," Lazaro said, "is much more terrible to experience, which makes the Garden a particularly fearful place to think about. The Second Death is the death of the spirit. Only an act of powerful magic can destroy your spirit. Man cannot kill a man's spirit no matter what he does to his body, because spirit is much stronger than earth. That's the basic fact of the act around this place, Ace."

Michael frowned, leaning his elbows on the table to peer at the little wizard better. Death of the spirit. He'd never felt even close to that before. No matter what else had happened to him, Michael had always had faith that his spirit would stay strong. For his spirit to die...he didn't even want to imagine what that might be like.

Lazaro paused to let his words sink in, then continued.

"Myself, I don't think it is possible to destroy a man's spirit, but that's just my own belief. There are those who fight with me about it, oh, yes, you can bet on that, old hat! I suppose you must decide for yourself what you believe, and what you are willing to risk. If Lord Striker really has the power to inflict the Second Death in his garden, that could be real bad news, you hear what I'm saying? So be very careful in your pursuit of your heart. You might think you can make it through anything, but Striker disagrees."

There was a long moment of silence between them, then Lazaro got up with a deep sigh and waved to Michael to follow him. Michael rose and followed the wizard back through the dining hall to a little door that led outside. There was a small patio with a hammock made of rope tied between a pair of old cottonwood trees. Next to the hammock was a wooden picnic table. Michael could picture the wizard reclining out here, relaxing safe in his castle walls with the wind rustling the trees overhead.

Lazaro gestured to the hammock. "You'd best rest, Chester. Long journey ahead, yessir."

Michael had to admit he was bone-tired. He climbed into the hammock. How long had it been since he'd had a moment to sit and just deal with everything, to rest? And the hammock was so comfy....

"What are you going to do?" Michael asked the wizard.

"Don't worry about me. I'll sleep right here on the grass. You ain't able, Mabel, but I do it all the time. I can sleep anywhere, anytime, start with a fart and stop on a dime."

Lazaro lay down on the ground, shuddered, sighed, and relaxed, his body and melon head seeming to settle and squash out like sagging clay. In seconds, he fell fast asleep, and began to snore with a sound like a pig gargling pancake batter. Michael watched him for a moment, half thinking it was a joke, but the little wizard snored on.

Michael lay back in the hammock and stared up through the leaves of the trees. He'd come so far, lost all track of time since he'd slipped into Shook. For all he knew it had been days that he'd gone without sleep. At the thought of sleep, he realized how heavy his eyelids felt, and he gave a huge yawn. He might as well take advantage of the opportunity to rest in a safe place. The hammock swayed gently back and forth and soon rocked him to sleep.

Not a single dream or vision disturbed Spirit Man while he slept in the hammock tied to the old cottonwood trees. It was as deep and restful a sleep as he had ever known.

When he awoke, he stretched and yawned, rubbed his eyes to clear them and then looked around, trying to place where he was. In an instant, he leapt up, promptly lost his balance, and fell out of the hammock. There was no one around. There was no five-story brown stone castle, no pipestone walks, and no Lazaro Hitchcock. The sun was setting behind the distant rolling hills and the Wizard of Shook was gone. Michael cursed himself for dropping his guard. There were so many more questions he had wanted to ask Lazaro. For starters: Do you have any swords?

On the upside, at least he felt refreshed and healthy, his stomach still full, and his head clearer now that he'd had some rest. That would certainly help with whatever was coming next.

The cottonwood trees stood alone in the middle of a clearing in the woods. The clearing was otherwise empty, except for one thing. A few yards away from him stood a gold door, at least eight feet tall, with scrolls and cherubs carved all around it. No sixteenth-century palace ever had a grander one. It gleamed in the dim sunset light of the clearing as if it was well cared for, like someone had just come through and polished it all for Michael's first sight of it.

Michael approached the door cautiously. Beautifully engraved in its gold face were the words: "DON'T BELIEVE IN WHAT YOU SEE." Yeah, he was beginning to get that message. With clenched jaw, he took a deep breath and grasped the gold doorknob.

The door swung away from him, nearly pulling him through and revealing a cloud of mist. The mist parted, exposing none other than the blue-robed figure of Lord Striker, still holding the crystal jar with Michael's heart in the bottom of it. Before Michael could catch his breath and move or say a word, Striker spoke.

"Don't bother throwing another rock. I'm only checking in on your progress. Not much, it seems, not much."

Michael's hands curled into fists but he restrained himself. Throwing a punch would do no good, and it might be exactly what Lord Striker wanted him to do. Inside the doorway, he couldn't see anything more than the dark mist and Striker himself, his blue robes swirling softly in the moving fog.

"I understand you had a productive chat with Lazaro," Lord Striker said with a grin. "Learn anything fun?"

"I learned that you're insane," Michael said. "And that the residents of Shook will rejoice when I cut you down."

Lord Striker feigned shock and held the crystal decanter to his chest, directly above his own rotten heart.

          HEART OF THE SPIRIT MAN

"It sounds as if you learned nothing, then," he said. "Because I think what Lazaro was trying to tell you, if I may be so bold, is that things are rarely as simple as they appear." He grinned with pointed teeth, his nose seeming to shift into the muzzle of a lion. "Besides, if you want to defeat the lion, you must do it in his den." He opened his mouth and it gaped like a lion's jaws, filled with deadly teeth and a great pink tongue. Then he extended one long finger and pointed toward Michael's chest.

"But you'd better get here quickly," he said. "You look like you're running out of time."

Michael looked down and saw, to his horror, that the discoloration had grown while he slept. It had spread almost to his collarbone and as far down as his abdomen. He touched it with his fingertips and recoiled. He was turning to stone.

"Well," Lord Striker said. "I'd best be going now. So much to do. So very much."

With a move like a diver doing a back layout, he raised his arms and dived backwards into the darkness behind him, disappearing once more with Michael's heart in his hands.

This time Michael didn't hesitate. With the mad resolve of a man leaping out of an airplane without a parachute, he ducked his shoulders and dived headfirst into the darkness behind the golden door.

Chapter 1

He wasn't falling, exactly, but neither was Michael standing on solid ground. Instead, he was just sort of...hovering. Or drifting. Or something else he didn't have the words for. He had to gasp for air at first, but soon found a way to regulate his breathing. The space around him appeared once again to be absolutely dark, but the curious thing was that he could see his own body clearly. Not darkness, then. This place was well-lit yet utterly empty. Beyond his hands and feet, a flat dimensionless void stretched on forever. Not black, but void like the sensation of trying to see with your toes. He tried to turn and look in all directions, but either he couldn't actually move or else everything in every direction was exactly the same. Left and right, up and down, all these became meaningless in that great emptiness.

Then, all at once, the emptiness ceased being empty. A blinding flash of blue light exploded across his retinas, showering him with stars that flashed across his vision. It was so bright that he thought he must have been struck by a firework or something similar, rather than only light. The burst left behind a tingling sensation and a strange taste in his mouth. Ozone? Whatever had happened, he now found himself resting against a perfectly flat and hard surface. His ears rang and his head ached terribly.

He didn't know if that flash had knocked him unconscious or awake, if he had been existing in the void for seconds or hours, or if he had been comatose for weeks. However long it had been, that was over now. The world rushed upon him. Sounds, warmth, color. He opened his eyes and immediately snapped them shut again, wincing against the brightness of the sunlit sky. His hands clawed at hot sand, and he sat upright. Carefully, he opened his eyes to slits and took a peek around, one hand over his eyes to protect them

     HEART OF THE SPIRIT MAN

from the bright light as much as possible.

Michael was sitting exactly in the middle of a crossroad where two perfectly straight dirt roads met before continuing on to the horizon in all four directions. Broken and rusted-out streetlights dangled from dark cables overhead, swinging back and ever so slightly. Michael saw no power lines, nothing to indicate that the road had been used in a very, very long time. The sand on which he sat was the rust-red of his home in New Mexico, and as far as he could see, it was heaped in mounds by the clumps of mesquite which grew through it.

The place looked almost like the Jornada back home, with the obvious difference that here, no mountains broke up the horizon, neither the Organs nor the Robledos.

The blazing sun hovered directly overhead. High noon. Yet he barely felt the heat on his skin. Sweat ran down his back so clearly his body was not immune to the blazing sun—he simply lacked the ability to feel it. He cast about for any sign of shelter or shade but found none. The broken street lights made a tiny, just-perceptible squeaking sound as they swung back and forth in the thick, sweltering breeze.

Michael stood up, kicking red sand into the air around him with his movement.

"Where's the sign?" he said to himself. Weren't crossroads supposed to have a sign? Then, as though in answer to his question, he saw them—four tiny signs low to the ground, just sticking up out of the sand along all four roads. Had they been there, before he asked his questions? Or had they really appeared in response to his words? It was always hard to tell, in Shook, what was within his control and what was not.

He knelt and read the first sign, which said, "YOU CAN GO FORWARD." The words shimmered as though they were a mirage. All four roads bore the exact same sign.

"Not very helpful," he muttered. Then he took a deep breath, coughed the dust from his mouth and blew it from his nose, and picked a direction. In just a few steps, he picked out another sign which read, "IN ANY DIRECTION." Michael picked up his pace and jogged to the next sign on the road. It read, "BUT YOU CAN'T GO BACK." His pace broke and he slowed to a halt. He looked back and the crossroad itself had vanished, only a long ribbon of road stretching back and back until it disappeared into the distant edge of the sky.

Of course. What else should he have expected? He took a few more steps and then stopped, taking stock of his situation. Even though he could barely feel the heat, his body would soon need water. His skin would burn. He needed to find a way out of this wasteland. The sun held its position directly over his head, his shadow only a tiny pool under his feet. What if it remained like that at all hours of the day? How was he to know how time worked in this corner of Shook?

He glanced at the sign again and cocked his head. He could continue down the road in the direction he was already going, or turn and see what waited in the opposite direction. Then again, he had never been one for only two options.

He stepped off the road and started walking across the desert.

The hot wind blew across the mesquite-studded red sands. It was almost unfair to call it wind—it was more like a dense, scalding fluid that flowed by in unsteady swirls. It sucked the water from his skin almost on contact, so although he was sweating heavily, his skin was never even moist at all. He had to admit that there was a certain comfort in the familiarity of the scene, as though he actually was back in New Mexico, and could feel almost at home in spite of the fact that he was quite lost. The comfort was quickly offset by his recollection that the rolling sea of sand there was called the Jornada del Muerte—the Journey of Death—because people had often died trying to cross it.

Michael tried not to dwell upon the fact that he had no water, though his dry mouth reminded him constantly of it. He trudged along with his head down, protecting his eyes from the glare, feeling the sweat running down the back of his neck. Hours passed with no sign of life, no sign of change. Michael looked up to see if the blazing sun had moved in the sky at all and it had not. This was a land of perpetual brutality, unwavering in its rejection of life.

Michael stumbled and nearly fell, but caught himself before he tipped over entirely. The texture of the ground had changed. Without realizing it, he had stumbled across another road. Was it the same road? Michael found himself standing again in the center of a crossroads with broken streetlights swinging lazily overhead. But there were no footprints in the direction from which Michael had come. No sign that he had come from anywhere at all, really.

Michael groaned and shouted at the desert sun, "Thanks! Really, thank you!"

If anything heard him, there was no indication of it.

Just when he thought he might have to begin the whole arduous trek over again in a different direction, something changed. The dust around his feet trembled a little, and before long he felt it too—a faint but distinct rumbling somewhere far away...and getting closer. That was new.

He squinted down the road, in the direction of the noise. Right at the point where it met the horizon, he spotted a little plume of dust. Tiny, distant, but quickly getting bigger.

He watched it a few seconds, then chuckled and nodded.

"Well, here comes fate," he said. Any change at this point would be better than the endless, burning desert. He stood in the center of the crossroads to wait for whatever it was to arrive. Then he laughed to himself. What was he doing? Lord Striker had made him too cautious by half. Spirit Man wasn't one to just wait around for things to happen. When he saw a chance at adventure, he went toward it!

He set off at a light jog toward the growing red-yellow cloud, watching the churning dust advance on him down the sandy desert road and hoping whatever it was would be friendly. Though it had at first appeared miles away, the cloud was rapidly closing the distance and must have been moving at a tremendously high speed. But what on earth—or on Shook—was it?

The answer came soon enough. Squinting for a better look as

he jogged, he was finally able to make out the gleam of metallic paint. Was that…a car? No, bigger than a car. It was a bright yellow Hummer! It seemed absurd in this landscape of dreams, but there it was, all roaring engines and whirring tires, a gaudy artifact of a bygone era. No sooner had Michael identified the vehicle than the space between them closed completely. The Hummer whizzed right past him, kicking up a huge cloud of dust that left him coughing and wheezing in its wake.

Still coughing, Michael waved his arms and ran after the vehicle.

"Hey!" he shouted. "Hey! Come back here!"

For a moment, he thought the driver hadn't noticed him at all, but a second later, brake lights appeared through the haze and a great grinding, screeching sound announced the driver had slammed on the brakes. Michael grinned with relief. He was willing to bet almost anything that the Hummer had air conditioning. With positively record-breaking speed, he ran to catch up with the chrome behemoth. As he got nearer to the car, a heavy, strong wind began to blow from behind him, pushing the dust that had been stirred past Michael and urging him on ever faster until he nearly crashed into the driver's side door.

A woman sat in the driver's seat, lifting her goggles up to peer back at him. She had large, dark eyes fringed by heavy eyelashes. She raised an eyebrow at him, evaluating him even as he evaluated her. Her thick black hair was threaded with the red dust she'd been driving through. She wore work boots, dusty jeans, and a battered white tank top smeared with grease and oil.

"Thought you were going somewhere else, sweetheart," she said, settling her goggles like a headband in her hair. The way she called him "sweetheart" sounded more like a question, or a challenge, than a term of endearment.

He swallowed hard. He probably would have felt his heartbeat quicken right then, if he'd had a heart.

"I didn't know any better," Michael said. "I'd just like to get out of this damn desert." Something in the cool way she regarded him, like he was no more interesting than the sand surrounding them, made him feel humble.

She tilted her head to one side, thoughtfully considering him. He glanced down at himself and had a brief thought that he wished he could have gotten a shower before meeting her. He was drenched in sweat, covered in dust, and all around looked like an absolute mess. After a moment that felt eternal, she sighed and jerked her thumb to the passenger seat. "Guess you'd better get your skinny ass in, then. I'm the only one coming this way for days. The only one you'd want to meet, at least." She pulled the goggles back down over her eyes, and he realized she hadn't rolled her window down, but that in fact the Hummer had no windows. At least, not anymore.

Michael thanked her, went around the car, and climbed into the passenger seat. Below his feet was a big toolbox, and he moved carefully so as not to kick it. The woman barely even waited for the door to shut before she hit the gas. Michael was thrown back in his seat with a gasp as they shot down the road again. He buckled up quickly.

"How'd you get out here, stranger?" she said, yelling over the braying of the engine. "Nobody comes this way but me and them."

"Them? Who are they?" Michael yelled back. It was a good thing the road was a straight shot—at the speeds they were accelerating to, he wasn't sure they could take a curve without flipping and tumbling across the sand.

"You better hope you don't find out." She laughed. "You don't look like you have the mettle for it, no 'fense." Her hair flew back in the wind and Michael found it difficult not to study her as they drove. She wasn't like anyone he had ever met, especially not in Shook. Nearly everyone he encountered here knew of him, or of Spirit Man, and had pretty strong feelings about him one way or another. But this woman? She barely even registered his existence. Didn't so much as glance at him when he was sitting a couple feet away from her. Who was she? Where had she come from?

"If you're gonna hitch a ride with me and Lemon Pie here," she said, reaching a hand out the window and patting the side of the Hummer, "I suppose we'll need to know your name, won't we?"

"Uh, Michael," he said. "You can call me Michael." It felt like a lie not to let her know he was Spirit Man—surely she would know that name, even if she didn't know his face—but he liked the idea of being anonymous in her eyes. Just some wanderer she found on the side of the road. "And you are?"

The edge of her mouth twitched in a smile. "My name is Solitaire," she said, "but folks call me Ace." She turned to look at him and Michael bit back a yell about watching the road. "So pretty boy, are you holding back already?"

"Sorry?"

"Just because I'm not fawning over you doesn't mean I don't know who you are, Spirit Man."

Damn.

"Oh, right," he said. He chuckled, trying to play it off. "I wasn't trying to withhold anything, I just figured it went without saying."

"Sure." She didn't sound like she believed him. "First strike, sweetheart. I like honesty." She grinned at him. "So don't hold back."

Her tone was half-serious, half-teasing. It put him on edge a little, but not necessarily in a bad way. Michael couldn't help but return her smile and nod.

"I won't. From here on, honesty's the policy." He turned his attention back to the road. It was much nicer to be in the car, with the wind whipping by and a roof over his head, but the road still looked endless, stretching on into forever.

"So," he said. "If I had continued the way I was going, where was I headed?"

"Middle of nowhere, where else?"

"I thought that's where I was already." Everything since he'd entered Shook, except for Lazaro's house, had felt like he was in the middle of nowhere.

"Things are like that here in Shook," she said, nodding. "But believe me, you ain't seen nothing yet. There are places out here that make this desert look like New York City."

"I find that hard to believe."

"Do I look like a liar to you?"

He shifted uncomfortably in his seat. "Uh, that's not—what I meant was—"

She laughed. "I'm messing with you, relax. Look, I already know you're aiming to take down the big Lord Strike-Out himself. And, lucky for you, I actually have a few leads on how to track down his hideout. So I'm going to take you to my place and then we're going to look for the Tower of Views and that secret garden of his."

"The Garden of Two Deaths," he said. The name sent chills down his spine despite the oppressive heat. "You might know how to get there?" He wasn't sure if he wanted her to say yes or no.

"Well, maybe. We'll see."

He almost asked her how she knew all these things, but it wasn't the first time and it certainly wouldn't be the last. Knowledge in Shook flowed differently than it did back on earth. It sort of sloshed back and forth across the land, refusing to stay in one spot—or one person's head—for very long. Besides, he hadn't drawn Ace by chance; there was more going on than he could know. If he had learned anything over his journeys, it was that it wouldn't help anything to question too much.

Still, he couldn't help asking after a few minutes of silence, "Why are you helping me?"

Ace shrugged, one hand on the wheel, the other draped out the window, drumming on the outside of the car.

"Do you ever think," she said after a long moment, "that there are things we're supposed to do?" She pulled her arm back into the car and reached down by her leg. She pulled up a big jug of water and handed it to him.

Gratefully, he took a swig. There were slices of lemon in it, somehow still fresh, giving the water a tangy sweetness.

"You don't ask a storm why it rains," she said, "or a desert why it's dry. It just is, and we accept it and go on." She stuck her hand out the window again, wiggling it up and down like a fish swimming in the dusty wind. "Here in Shook, we all have our roles to play. Some of us are wizards and some are clowns and some are lords. Me, I'm Ace, and I've got my own place." She laughed at the accidental rhyme.

"Isn't that reason enough, sweetheart?"

Maybe it was. They drove on in silence.

Chapter 8

Michael kept his eyes out the windows, watching the desert stream around them like a dusty river. Occasionally he took a swig from the jug, and now and then Ace did, too, which always made Michael a little nervous considering their velocity. Ace drove at positively maniac speeds, tearing up the dusty road beneath her tires. But she hadn't crashed yet. Might as well sit back and see where she was driving them.

After a long silence, Ace was the one to break it.

"All right, penny for your thoughts," she said.

"What?"

"Okay, I'll go first. Pain is to pleasure as darkness is to light," she quoted, though he didn't know what from. "How's that? What do you think it means?"

"Maybe that you can't have one without the other?" he ventured.

"Yeah, maybe," she said. "So does it mean pain is like the absence of pleasure? Because that doesn't sound right to me. Besides, you can have both at once, can't you?" She tilted a smile at him, like she was testing him, or playing some kind of game.

"Are you disagreeing with it now? You're the one who came up with it."

"Not really. I just sort of picked it out of the air." She made a plucking gesture with her fingers, like she was catching a dandelion seed caught on the wind.

He started to ask what that meant, exactly, but before he could say a word, Ace looked into her rearview mirror and swore.

"Shit, piss, and corruption! We've got ourselves some unwanted company, Spirit Man."

Michael turned around to look out the back window and saw a band of ragged bikers tailing them. Some had bright blue and blood red banners flying from their bikes, and the dust they stirred up in their wake spiraled into the sky.

"Who the hell are they?" he said.

"Strikers," she spat, with both contempt and a certain fear in her voice.

"I'm assuming they work for Lord Striker?"

"That's a generous way to put it. More like they're his fanatical lackeys. Hell, they're so dedicated to that asshole that they give up their own names and take his."

The motorcycle tires slashed across the desert road. Despite Ace's frankly unsafe speed, the Strikers were gaining on them. They wore black leather jackets with gold and silver chains, and bright red pants. Gold bandanas covered up half of their faces, like they were punk imitations of Lord Striker himself. They hooted and hollered loud enough to make a racket even over the roar of the Lemon Pie's engine.

"They're catching up to us," Michael said.

Ace dropped a gear and made a sharp left turn off the road. With expert precision, she twisted and swerved between the mesquite hummocks, flinging Michael this way and that as she changed direction on a dime. Michael was glad he'd put on his seatbelt at least. They zigzagged across a flat stretch of red sand, kicking up a cloud of red dust to blind the Strikers and carving deep skid-ruts into the earth to throw their bikes off balance.

"How many of them we got, sweetheart?" Ace asked as she stomped the pedal to the floor.

"Forty, fifty maybe, I don't know! I can't see through the dust." The wind had picked up as well, swirling the dust kicked up by all those angry tires in a vortex around the Hummer and the motorcycles both. The Strikers appeared utterly unfazed, and rode through that sand-whipping gale without so much as flinching.

"I sure hope you know a way out of here, Ace," he said, trying to control the nerves creeping into his voice. "These ugly bastards are right on our ass!"

Ace nodded, then stuck her hand out the window and raised her middle finger at the bikers with a billowing laugh. Just then, the Hummer broke out of the swirling dust, struck a hummock, and went airborne, flying over a clump of mesquite. Michael couldn't hold back a scream of terror as they soared through the air. They landed with a jolt Michael felt in every bone of his body, then Ace kept right on driving.

"All right!" she crowed as the vehicle bounced at last onto a stretch of paved road. "Now we're getting somewhere! That's the Cisceron Gorge Bridge about a quarter of a mile up there ahead." She pointed down the road, but Michael was too caught up in trying to blink the dust out of his eyes to see anything.

The Strikers were also turning onto the road, though their numbers had significantly dwindled. It looked like all of Ace's fancy maneuvering had accomplished something after all. She looked in the rearview mirror and smirked.

"Have I got a big surprise for you lot!" she shouted.

Michael couldn't imagine what use a bridge could be in the middle of this flat desert, but soon they passed a road sign that read: "CISCERON GORGE BRIDGE. DREAM ON, YOU FOOLS, DREAM ON."

And just like that, the gorge appeared as if from nowhere. The desert fell away along steep, towering bluffs as the Hummer cruised onto an enormous steel cable suspension bridge which spanned the length of that chasm. Michael hazarded a look down to see what must have been the mighty Cisceron River rushing fiercely through a narrow canyon far below.

"Wouldn't recommend looking down," Ace said. Then she reached down beside her seat and pulled up a short lever. "Look out the back instead."

From two pipes at the back of the truck came two black sprays of oil, which spread in a sheet to cover the entire bridge.

"Like freaking Batwoman, huh?" she said.

A dozen Strikers rode their big motorcycles onto the bridge, six abreast. The leader raised his front wheel up off the road in a wheelie and zoomed forward, hooting at the top of his lungs. His elation quickly turned to a cry of panic as he hit the slick oil patch. The bike lurched back and forth, then crashed into the bike beside him, and then into another. As the first row crashed and spun out, the second row slammed into them, sending bikes and Strikers tumbling madly across the bridge. At least four or five Strikers went hurtling over the guardrails along the sides of the road and plunged to their deaths in the white-water rapids of the river.

"Any more back there?" Ace said.

"Quite a few," Michael said. They may have been slipping around in the oil slick and looking pretty comical at the moment, but they looked mad as hell and he didn't want to know what they would do once they got back on their bikes.

"Not a problem," said Ace. She grabbed a long red flare from beneath her seat and pulled off the trigger cap with her teeth. Then she threw it out the window. In very slow motion, Michael watched the red flare soar up into the sky and then fall through the air until it landed directly in the middle of the oil slick. For a moment, nothing. The Strikers stopped dead in their tracks and looked at the flare with wide eyes. Then a huge burst of fire and black smoke swept outward and engulfed them. Strikers screamed as they caught fire, rolling around to try to put out the blaze but succeeding only in covering themselves with more oil. Even knowing that they would certainly have killed both Michael and Ace if they had caught up with them, it was a hard sight to watch. Perhaps mercifully, the fire proved too much for the bridge itself, and it began to groan and buckle in the heat. Ace jammed the accelerator and the Hummer emerged onto solid ground just as the whole bridge crumpled and went tumbling down to the bottom of the Cisceron Gorge.

Ace cheered wildly and bounced up and down in her seat with unrestrained glee.

"Gotcha!" she shouted in delight. "Don't pick a fight with the Ace, kids."

"I certainly wouldn't pick a fight with you," Michael said. "You're one tough cookie." It was true. She'd been so...*joyful* in destroying those Strikers that it was hard to imagine going up against her.

Definitely not a good idea.

"You got that right, sweetheart. Now, have you had enough adventure for one day, Spirit Man? You look fit to piss your pants."

"Yeah, no more surprises, please, or I fear for Lemon Pie's seat covers."

They both laughed.

"Hey, listen," Ace said. "I know of a quiet place not far from here. It's the City of Rocks, a nice place to camp and spend the night. The moon is full tonight so there will be plenty of light. How does that sound to you, Spirit Man?"

The idea of resting after a day like today was pure bliss. Michael nodded. "Sounds perfect."

"Of course it does, it was my idea," she teased. "You go ahead and try to get some shut-eye. It's a couple hours' drive from here still. No use in both of us being up, and I'll be damned if anyone but me drives the Lemon Pie."

Michael leaned back in his seat. He couldn't deny that he was feeling profoundly worn out. As the adrenaline of their encounter with the Strikers subsided, exhaustion took its place. The instant he closed his eyes, he fell fast asleep.

He was jolted awake by the car bumping over a pothole a few hours later. Ace was heading down a skinny one-lane road that looked like it had definitely seen better days. Up ahead, a great purple arch rose from the desert, its polished surface reflecting the fiery sunset playing out along the western horizon. Little light bulbs flickered on the arch, spelling out "The City of Rocks, an Ephemeral State Park of the Ninth Diocese of Shook" in elegant script. There really was no end to this world, was there?

Ace parked the car in front of the arch. She elbowed Spirit Man to wake him more fully.

"Look alive, sleeping beauty. Welcome to the City of Rocks. Check out that amazing sunset. Take it all in while you've got the time to breathe."

While he had time to breathe? What an odd way to put it. Michael sat up and rubbed the sleep from his eyes. He still felt groggy as he looked across the wide valley that stretched in front of him. Bizarre, alien rock formations stretched all around him for miles and miles in every direction. Twisting arches, spindly hoodoos, jagged fins, and bulbous constructions he didn't even have the words for, all glowing in the setting sun, their shadows long and haunting as they reached across the desert landscape. Michael sat there in total silence as he absorbed the boundless beauty of this strange land.

"A long, long time ago, there was a huge volcano not far from here," Ace said. "The eruption sent all these rocks flying across the sky, and somehow they all ended up here, stacked on top of one another like this." She paused for a moment and then added, "Or maybe it was a big dragon that nested here and breathed fire and smoke across the land when he was displeased. Really depends on where you get your stories, I suppose." She shifted into drive and they puttered through the arch, the Hummer's engine a low purr now that they weren't rocketing along that everlasting road.

As they drove, Michael started to see shapes in the rocks, as one might see them in the clouds above. There was one which looked like a duck dipping its head into a pond or stream. And there beyond it was what looked like a camel with two huge rocky humps. He pointed these out to Ace, but she didn't agree with his assessment.

"A duck? That's clearly a rabbit. And those two humps over there look like a camel to you? Come on, boy, anyone can see that's a woman dancing. Do you see her heels?"

They went back and forth like this for quite a while, apparently unable to agree on a single interpretation of the rocks they saw. It took him an embarrassingly long time to realize she was messing with him again, inventing new shapes on the fly just to disagree with him.

"What happened to honesty?" he said.

She cracked up first, then he did too, unable to keep a straight face. It seemed they had the place all to themselves. There were no other campers here, no people drinking beer or playing loud music which would disturb their neighbors and shatter the deafening sound of silence in this eerie place. None of the interruptions Michael was used to in places like this, distractions from the world. Michael felt that the road, and the concrete picnic tables, were just other natural features, and no one had ever been there before he and Ace arrived. It felt almost as if the earth itself had created this little campground, as natural as the ocean or a volcanic eruption.

Ace rounded a bend of the dirt road and pulled into a campground with a picnic table and a small shelter made of tin sheets on a metal frame. As though she had known exactly where she intended to park all along, she pulled in and turned off the engine.

"You've heard of a five-star hotel?" she said. "Well, you're not going to believe the number of stars this place has."

They stepped out of the car. In the waning twilight Michael could read a park sign that had been secured in the dirt with large wooden stakes. Painted on a sheet of metal, it had once been white, but the sun had yellowed the paint and rust had browned the steel. The words had once been black, but time had reduced them to faded brown. At the top, it said simply: "PARK RULES." Beneath in block letters, it read: "Please keep the dream alive, and please put all your trash in the receptacles provided." Michael smiled, and felt very reassured that he was where he was supposed to be, wherever that was. Someone had known he was going to come here, and a long time ago, by the look of the sign.

After making sure her car was taken care of, Ace knelt by an old fallen tree limb and gathered some dry pieces of firewood to make a campfire. Michael watched her for a time, still trying to understand this mysterious woman who seemed to know so much more than she would ever let on. He was aware, in some distant way, that if he had a heart, he might feel himself drawn to her out of more than just the necessity of his mission. It felt, in that moment, like an unimaginable loss. A chance at love squandered, suffocated before it could take its first breath by the cold, heavy stone in his chest. He tried not to let the deep sorrow that thought evoked show on his face.

Ace turned around and gave him a pointed glance. "Having fun? I could use some help over here, you know."

"Right!" he said, abashed, and jumped to help her. He gathered more firewood and helped her build the fire, starting with a big handful of dry desert grass, overlaying that with kindling, and finally propping bigger pieces in a pyramid over the whole thing. By the time they were finished, it was growing quite dark. Ace lit the grass, which lit the small twigs, which licked at the dry firewood, and in very short order they had a growing fire. The dancing fire reflected upon their faces.

Ace went to her Hummer and brought two sleeping bags out from a panel built into the back. He raised an eyebrow, wondering why she had two.

As if reading his mind, Ace said, "Always prepared, like a good Girl Scout. Never know when a sleeping bag might catch fire." She grinned and threw one of the bundles to him, spreading out the other on the clean desert sand beside the campfire. He spread out the other nearby and sat cross-legged on it. He tried to think of the last time he'd felt like he could truly relax, let down his guard, and just be for a while. Lazaro's castle, sure, but that had been different, in part because Lazaro was so unpredictable. Whoever Ace was, wherever she'd come from, she certainly had a calming energy about her.

Night fell in earnest across the desert. The firelight glowed across the car and the metal sign and the nearby rock formations. As the fire dwindled, Michael waited for their surroundings to fall completely into shadow and become all but invisible, but it didn't happen. Even once the fire was no more than faintly glowing embers, he could still make out the shapes of the great rocks around them with clarity. He looked up into the sky and gasped. He had never seen so many stars anywhere in the many worlds through which he had traveled. There were so many stars that their total light actually cast a soft glow that lit the world. Then, on the horizon, a small but very bright moon began to rise, casting a soft silvery glow as it climbed higher into the sky. Shadows reemerged in the light of the moon, and as that immense satellite moved across the sky, the shadows moved with it, making it appear that the great rock statues were alive and wriggling.

Michael raised his hands and made a shadow rabbit with his fingers. It was faint, but clearly discernible against the yellow side of the Lemon Pie. He followed this with a rooster, then a kangaroo. Ace watched him with an arched eyebrow as his long fingers twisted and curled and intertwined. He made a horse, an elephant, a dog. She chuckled at him, at his delight in simply making shadow creatures, and he blushed, embarrassed to have been doing something so childish.

"That's great," she said solemnly, "but did you know there are monsters roaming these parts?"

"Really?" Michael asked, once again alert for the faintest sound.

"Oh, certainly. Here, I can show you. I think there are some creeping nearby." Then she stood and made her own shadow figures, using not just her hands but her whole body. She cast them on the side of a huge, flat boulder. Her first one was a tall dragon, with a spiked tail. Then she bent down and made a cat with its back arched. But when she stood back up, the shadow became clearly and horribly none other than Lord Striker himself, robe billowing around him, his hand holding a lump that Michael knew had to be his heart, pulsing softly. He couldn't hold back a sharp gasp.

"Scared ya, didn't I?" Ace teased. The shadow melted away and became, once again, only hers. She laughed and sat down on her sleeping bag once again, no longer a monstrous god in the dark.

"Shook is a world filled with great pain and great beauty, Michael," she said. "Plenty of monsters, everywhere. Evil, heartless things. Most of them can't even feel a thing."

By instinct, Michael's hand went to his own chest. The stone was spreading. It covered nearly his entire ribcage now, replacing warm flesh with cold rock. His left shoulder, too, was turning. When he looked up again, Ace was watching him with deep, sad eyes.

"He said I was running out of time," Michael said.

She nodded. "If it spreads all the way...if it turns you completely... I don't think there's any coming back from that. We have to make sure that doesn't happen. This world can't afford to lose Spirit Man."

"Well," he said, trying to put on a brave face. "I'll just have to find that Garden of Two Deaths then, won't I?"

"You will. I know you will."

"What about the Strikers? Do you think they'll follow us here?"

"Nah," she said. "Not tonight anyway." She drank from the water jug and passed it to him. "They'll be held up fooling around with that bridge instead of coming another way."

"There's another way?"

"Sure. There's another way to get just about anywhere, if you're creative enough. You ought to know that more than anybody, Spirit Man." Ace lay back on her sleeping bag and looked up at the stars. When she spoke again, she did so softly, her voice as gentle as the light of the stars above.

"If Striker really is the god of this world, as he seems to think he is, then what does that mean about people like you and me? What if he really did create us, Michael? Long before anyone can remember. What if we really are just the creations of an insane, evil being like that?"

"I don't think it changes anything," Michael said. "I don't think it makes us anything like him."

But he wasn't sure if he really believed that. He saw the Strikers burning to death on the bridge, saw himself bleeding on the stone altar, saw innocent people bleeding in the diner as bullets whizzed by, saw his friend Mark bleeding for nothing, for a stupid hustle. If everyone really was in some way a child of Lord Striker, would that be so surprising? Everyone seemed capable of so much cruelty, so much violence—even Ace, even him. Didn't those things belong to Lord Striker? Couldn't they have come from him?

He stared into the emptiness of the lonely desert, the endless metropolis of misshapen stones, and thought of everyone he would never see again, everything he would never feel again, if he, too, became stone. Just another curiosity for parkgoers to point at and say "A man, I see a man!" The glitter of the stars above seemed cold now.

"The road ahead," Ace said after a long silence. "It's not going to be easy. You know all this. That's why we met. You know that things happen for a reason. You haven't met an accident in years, and I know it's not a revelation to you to hear that. Only, if I'm going to help you, if I'm going to make it my business to get you where you're going and help you get your heart back....I need to know that you understand what it's going to take. It might just take everything. More than you thought you could give."

Michael nodded but said nothing. The moon had grown fat, and looked exactly like the full moon above Mount Solitaire back home in New Mexico, back when he'd last left the world he knew for another one. Was this his fate, then? Never to stay, never to truly rest, only to move from one strange world to the next, one life or death struggle to the next?

"Good night, Spirit Man," Ace whispered. She reached out idly and patted his cheek before turning over and lying on her own sleeping back, her back to him. He turned away and thought of the soft warmth of her palm, which in another life might have stirred something in him but which now he barely even felt. Too much sorrow for one night. He closed his eyes beneath that sky full of stars and the white-faced moon and willed sleep to take him.

That night, as he sometimes did, Spirit Man dreamed within his dream. In the dream within a dream, he stood up from the sleeping bag and walked among the alien rocks beneath a full moon far larger than any he had ever seen. A rolling fog crept across the land as Spirit Man walked between the boulders, shrouding the landscape from sight. When the fog touched him, his entire body became white as snow. He examined himself and found that he looked exactly like a Striker. Somewhere, a heart was beating and pounding wildly, but he couldn't say where the sound was coming from, couldn't pick it out in all the fog.

Spirit Man ran to the top of a ridge as the heartbeat grew louder and louder, like a steady drumbeat pounding ceaselessly, drowning out all thoughts. He raised his hands up to the Shook sky and screamed as loud as he could. His voice echoed high up into the heavens and the heavens heard him. The sky peeled open and Spirit

Man saw, there in the night sky, Lord Striker holding the glass jar which held Michael's heart. All at once, the clamorous beating of the heart ceased and fell deathly silent. The world became very quiet all around him. Striker spoke to him but he couldn't understand the words. All he knew was that Lord Striker was speaking as if to a child—slowly and patiently and full of tenderness. That gentle voice forced a far deeper dread into him than any of Lord Strikers taunts had ever done and he tried to flee but found he could not move. His legs had turned to stone.

Then the little Wizard of Shook appeared at Lord Striker's side. This time, however, he wore the gold mask of a Striker and danced madly around the feet of the blue-robed giant. He leaped into the air, flipped over in a back flip, and knocked the glass vessel containing Michael's heart from Lord Striker's hand. The decanter fell through the star-filled sky and all Spirit Man could do was watch, powerless to stop its descent. It landed right on top of the camel rock and the whole thing, heart and decanter both, shattered into millions of tiny pieces. Gone for all time, never to be recovered. Spirit Man cried out, horrified beyond sensation. This was the second death, the final death.

Michael sat bolt upright in his sleeping bag, breathing hard. It was still deep night. Ace was still beside him. His legs had not yet turned to stone. His heart had not yet been destroyed. There was still hope. He needed to remember that there was still hope.

Tentatively, fearing another nightmare, he lay back down and let sleep reclaim him.

Chapter 9

It wasn't the silence that woke Michael, though that was the first thing of which he was conscious. He emerged from his dreams like rising up from deep water, slowly regaining buoyancy. He left his eyes shut at first, listening for the world around him for a long moment. The more he came into wakefulness, the less perfect the silence became. A bird was chirping in the distance, its notes forming a strange and uneven song. A sigh of wind came and went. Michael rolled to his back on the sleeping bag, rubbed his eyes, and opened them with a great yawn.

The sky was still black, but there were so many stars that the space between them seemed to have a texture of its own, like polished obsidian. To the east, he could see a hint of color, somewhere between crimson and violet. He watched it spread like a gaseous nebula across the sky, without any distinct edge, but ever-advancing. It was like watercolors bleeding across a starry canvas.

Then, the slow, cautious movement of it all rapidly picked up the pace. In what seemed like only seconds, the sky began to flame in swirls of red and gold, with slashes of chartreuse, heliotrope, turquoise, and coral twisting across the sky. It was unlike any sunrise Michael had ever seen. As the disc of the sun finally broke the horizon with a blaze of fire, Michael marveled that it in fact looked not so much like a sunrise as it did a recording of a sunset played backwards.

There was a soft noise from the other sleeping bag and he turned to see Ace stretching her arms over her head. She sighed, yawned, and sat up, rubbing her eyes with the heel of her hand.

"Dawn," she mumbled, yawning again.

He nodded, not yet ready to break the quiet of the morning. She rose, slipped on her boots, and went to poke the coals in the fire pit.

She dug a blue enamel coffee pot from the car, fixed it over the fire, and blew on the coals until they began to smoke. Then she dropped some fresh kindling onto the coals, waited for it to light, and followed with a few larger pieces of wood. A lively fire flared up within moments, and a short time later the pot boiled and let off a mellow whistle. A cloud of steam rose up around her, hanging in the morning air like a spirit, and with it came the delicious aroma of fresh coffee. She smiled and leaned over to inhale the smell more deeply.

Michael was glad she was still there, still herself and not some trick of Shook. As if she had forgotten he was there, she began to hum to herself and trotted over to her Hummer, rolling up her sleeping bag and tossing it in its appropriate place. He found himself wondering what Lord Striker was doing at this very moment, sequestered in his hidden lair. Somehow the idea of Striker having anything close to a human morning routine felt impossible to Michael. More likely he was boiling kittens in a big pot, or pouring over a big map of the dream world and moving around figures standing in for his various armies, or something else similarly villainous. What Lazaro had said…it just wasn't possible. There was no way that wicked giant had ever been anything close to human, anything at all like Spirit Man.

Ace pulled him from his thoughts. "Seems to be ready, Spirit Man," she said. "Would you like a cup of joe?"

"I thought you'd never ask." He stretched his back and shoulders before taking the big silver cup of hot coffee she brought him.

"I don't have any cream or sugar," she said. "Hope black is okay. I tend not to fuss over things like this."

"It's perfect," he said. And it was. It would be warm in the desert soon, but for now it was chilly enough still that the steam felt great, almost like stepping into a hot shower first thing in the morning. Emphasis on "almost." Michael didn't even want to think about how long it had been since he'd gotten the chance to shower.

"Any fun dreams?" Ace said, sipping her own coffee. Her expression was only one of polite curiosity. She was just trying to strike up a conversation, not probe into anything. He needed to stop being so paranoid all the time.

"Nothing I can make much sense of," he said after a moment. It wasn't exactly a lie, but it wasn't entirely the truth either. He didn't know why, but he couldn't bring himself to describe what he had seen, the shattering of his heart and the stone overtaking him. Somehow, he felt that if he said it aloud, he might bring these events into being. His chest felt simultaneously heavy and unbearably light, and he shifted the subject quickly.

"Where are we heading from here, then?" he said.

"Well, if we're going up against Lord Striker, we can't do that with our bare hands. I know a place where we can gear up a little, you know? Give ourselves a fighting chance."

Their conversation from the night before hung between them as they packed up their camp. By the time they were finished, the peaceful, dozy morning mood had turned into something more determined and focused, losing that blurry edge. They hopped back into the Hummer and wound back through the City of Rocks in silence. Michael took one last look at the place as they pulled once more onto the endless highway, then they left it behind for good.

Ace accelerated back to usual her manic speed and glanced over to Michael.

"The place is about four hundred miles from here," she shouted over the wind and the engine. "It'll take most of the day to get there."

Michael nodded and draped his arm out of the car, flattening his palm as if his hand was riding the wind streams around them, and watched the desert landscape stream by.

As they drove, the monotony of the desert gave way to an unbelievable breadth of scenery. Extinct volcano ranges loomed in the far distance, regal and imposing even in death. Tall, swaying palm trees surrounded deep blue lakes. Grassy plains rippled for miles upon miles. Sometimes Ace would point to something and recount a story of the last time she had been there. Often, these stories involved more than a little danger and risky driving, and it was hard to tell when she was being honest and when she was just trying to see exactly how much absurdity Michael would believe.

By midafternoon, tall plumes of smoke appeared in the distance, and before long they came to a tiny village in the middle of an otherwise unbroken desert. Ace slowed to a more reasonable speed to better see what had happened. A smoldering sign outside town announced the place as "Shakey Town." There were long rows of rundown shacks on both sides of the road that cut through the deserted town. Almost every single one was in flames, or else had already been reduced to a pile of smoking ashes. A thick blanket of black smoke covered the sky and the air was acrid with that dark haze. As Ace drove through the burning town, no sign of life showed itself anywhere. They reached the town center and parked in the main plaza they found there. Dozens of signs had been nailed up on the sides of the ruined buildings. Most of them were made from sheets of plywood, yet they remained remarkably intact, apparently untouched by the flames. One read, "It's nothing to fear, my dear!"

"Ace, what do you make of all these signs?" he said. He pointed to one that read, "What are you waiting for? Get going!" The signs unnerved him—he couldn't shake the feeling that they had been nailed up after the buildings had been set aflame. More than that, he couldn't help but feel that they had been left here for him to find.

"I don't know," Ace said with a frown. She pulled her goggles up and rested them on her brow so she could better see the damage around them. "I've never paid much attention to them. There are signs everywhere in Shook. If I stopped to care about or read all of them, I'd never leave home. I kind of like that one." She pointed to a sign that said simply, "Believe in me!"

He walked from one to the next, trying to parse whatever it was they were saying.

"Look within."

"Sometimes dreams really do come true."

"See you at the Garden."

"And the Tower of Views."

Ace approached and put a hand on his shoulder. "What do you make of it?" she said.

"Lord Striker," he said. "He wants me to know this was his doing."

They got back into the car. The longer they stayed in the town, the more uneasy Michael felt. He had a strong feeling that there was something even worse than all this ruin waiting just around the corner.

"I'll be glad to see the last of this place," Ace said as she threw the Hummer into drive. She pulled her goggles back over her eyes to shield them from the smoke and continued down the road.

Half a block later, she gasped and slammed on the brakes. Michael followed the line of her sight and his breath caught in his throat. There, in an empty lot beside one of the burned-out homes, lay a pile of smoldering corpses. Michael stepped out of the vehicle and walked closer to see if anyone could be helped. The smell of burning flesh assaulted his nostrils and he nearly vomited. He felt lightheaded, like he might collapse at any moment. Ace slid an arm around his waist to help support him as they walked around the dead, searching for any impossible signs of life. But of course, there were none. Everyone in Shakey Town was dead and burned, and all of them had their hearts ripped out of their chests in some crude approximation of what Lord Striker had done to Michael on top of Mount Solitaire.

Ace struggled for breath, her whole body trembling. "All these innocent people," she said. "Why?"

"To send a message," Michael said, and in saying it, he knew it was true. He saw it all play out in his mind's eye as if on a screen. The band of Strikers roaring down from the mountain behind the town, churning through that quiet community on their chrome motorcycles. Dragging people from their homes. Throwing Molotov cocktails through windows and hooting as the flames took. Cutting down every man, woman, and child they found with knives and axes and their own clawed hands. Tearing out their hearts so Michael would know exactly who this offering was made for. Throwing the bodies into this pile and setting fire to the whole lot to ensure there would be no survivors, not even one.

It was too much to think of, too much pain all piled into one place. The vision faded but slowly, far too slowly. Michael stared at Ace and she shook her head.

"It's not your fault," she said.

"Then why does it feel like it is?"

She embraced him and he hugged her back, as if holding on tightly for a moment would shield them from all this death. As if an embrace was enough to keep them from seeing what they had already seen. He felt Ace's breath against his neck.

"I've been through here before," she whispered softly. "They were good people, Michael. They didn't....Of course they didn't deserve this."

She pulled back at last and gently touched the stone creeping up his neck.

He flinched away, though he hadn't felt her fingertips at all. "We can't stay here," he said. "They might come back this way. We've got to get going."

They did not speak a word to each other as they left town. Michael fumbled with the radio. He found nothing but static filling the airwaves. Ace's whole demeanor had changed. Gone was the sly, teasing woman he had first met. In her place sat a somber, determined warrior. Neither of them needed to say what both of them were thinking. Lord Striker would pay for all that he had done. Not only in Shakey Town, but across the entire land of Shook. They would find a way to make him pay, no matter the cost.

There was that phrase again. "No matter the cost." It had been bouncing around Michael's head since he lost his heart and only now did he stop to examine it. Did he really believe that? Would he really do anything, anything, to punish Lord Striker for his sins? He felt almost certain that he would, and that scared him, in a way. Because of course there would be a price. There was always a price, whether on earth or in Shook. Everything costs. And here, without even seeing the price tag, he was agreeing to pay it.

Why, he wondered, was there such a need for death and destruction in this dream world? Was any of it really necessary when there was so much death and destruction in his own world back in New Mexico? What was all the hating and suffering and dying for? Or, perhaps more importantly, who was it for? What could possibly be the divine purpose or rational reason to kill any living thing at all, for that matter? For any god of any world, to be a mass murderer of his own people could only be purely evil and unforgivable—couldn't it? Maybe it was more complicated than that, but he didn't understand how it could be. People on earth died and were killed every day, after all, since the beginning of time. The problem of suffering, he remembered someone calling it once, though he couldn't recall if they had ever offered a solution for such a problem. Weren't gods, whether here in Shook or back on earth, the reason for death itself? What were they thinking when they created suffering and pain and sadness and tears? Could the nihilists be right in complaining that a god gives life only to snatch it away in the blink of an eye? One breath and then gone like dust in the wind. What had the ancient Greeks thought of all this? The Vikings? The great philosophers of the east? He didn't know. And even if he had known, he somehow doubted he would have found any of their answers satisfactory.

As they drove, Michael found hot tears running down his cheeks. He hoped Ace wouldn't notice and didn't move to wipe them away, for fear that she would see. It was childish, of course, to hope to hide his emotions like that, but she looked so strong, so stoic, that he couldn't imagine what she would think of him if she saw his tears. He stared out the window in an effort to hide his face from her.

"I've spent too long in the desert," she said. "Too long conserving moisture. Otherwise I'd weep too, Spirit Man. It's nothing to be ashamed of."

So he let the tears continue flowing, blearing the landscape as it whirred past. He thought of the wizard Lazaro Hitchcock and what he'd said about the Garden of Two Deaths. The first death is only the death of the flesh, but the second death, the second death of the spirit, was so much harder to inflict. It was a strangely comforting thought. Maybe despite the violence of the Strikers and their cruel Lord, something of Shakey Town might remain beyond their bodies, beyond the little town in the Shook desert. It wasn't much, but it was better than nothing.

He glanced again at Ace in the seat beside him. Her eyes were fixed firmly on the road. She barely even blinked. Where had she come from, for her to take this death so easily? She'd been so casual about lighting those Strikers on fire, and now this. He didn't know if her steadiness comforted him or if it unsettled him. It was probably good that one of them was unshaken, but still, he didn't know what to make of her lack of reaction. It was almost like she was the one made of stone, rather than him.

Two-and-a-half hours down the highway, they came to a wide intersection that appeared to have been the victim of a rockslide, though there were no mountains nearby. Huge boulders were strewn across the pavement, blocking all four roadways. Ace slowed down and then brought the powerful vehicle to a stop. They idled there for a moment without speaking. In the center of that blocked intersection stood a door.

"I take it this isn't quite where we were going?" Michael said.

"No, not exactly."

"But it's where we need to go."

"That does tend to be the way these doors work, at least in my extensive experience."

The door was no larger than an average house door, white with a shiny brass knob. There was an old wooden sign hanging from it, bearing antique letters which read, "SEBASTIAN SPIRIT."

Ace put on the parking brake and the two of them stepped out of the Hummer and walked over to the mysterious door.

"Any idea where it might take us?" he said.

"Not a clue. But considering we're a little short on time, I'd wager it's probably our best option, uncertainty be damned."

Michael started to reach out to touch the doorknob, then hesitated. He wondered if the right move might not be to just get back into the Hummer with Ace and drive away in any direction. They could keep driving for hours, see everything the desert had in store for them. Hell, they didn't even need to find Lord Striker, did they? They could just drive and drive and drive. The Hummer, despite its reputation, seemed to never need fuel, so what was to stop them from just cruising off into the sunset and leaving all this nasty work

     HEART OF THE SPIRIT MAN

behind? But his stone heart was growing heavier. He didn't have all the time in the world anymore.

"Let's just take a peek," he said. "We can see what's through it and then make our decision."

He reached out toward the brass doorknob. The instant his fingers touched it, however, the entire door disappeared in a blink, and Michael was sucked into the hole like a mosquito caught by a vacuum cleaner. He tried to scream, but his voice was literally frozen in his throat. The last thing he saw before disappearing into another world was Ace shouting, reaching a hand out to catch him, and not quite making it.

His body jerked to a tense bow as swirling winds drove subzero blasts of ice crystals into his skin. He tumbled through blinding white frozen space, whipped and twirled by the fierce blizzard. He was up in the air again, tossed about in some kind of polar vortex. Then, terrifyingly, the wind lifted for a second and he felt himself being dropped. His body jerked itself into a fetal cannonball as he plummeted, and he hugged his knees tight to his chest and waited for the end.

The end, as it turned out, came in the form of a huge snowbank. He plowed into it and came to a stop buried in frigid white powder. It was over before he fully realized it had begun, and his first real awareness of the event was that it was over, and he had survived. The answer to his next question—how deep he was buried—came when he tried to sit up, tossed the snow from his arms, and discovered himself sitting in the bottom of a crater blasted six feet into the snow.

He crawled to the rim of the crater and took a look around. Everything he could see was white and swirling. Apart from being able to see where he was putting his feet, he might as well have been blind. By crouching down in the crater, he could give himself a bit of protection from the freezing winds. As with the sun's heat, he felt the cold only in a distant way, but since he was still dressed in the jeans and shirt he wore in the desert, he knew he would freeze to death in minutes there.

Blinking off the icicles forming on his eyelashes, he hefted himself up out of the crater and began walking in the direction he was blown by the wind. Soon his feet started going completely numb and he tripped and fell frequently, unable to control his balance. After one particularly bad fall, he pushed himself up with a snarl and shouted into the screaming wind.

"Is this it? Is this the best you have? You think this will stop me from ripping out your heart?"

Just then, he felt something hard protruding from the snow. For a split second, the wind cleared the surface of the snow away and Michael could see before him a flight of black stone steps leading steeply up into the depthless white mass of the arctic storm. Michael struggled to his feet and tried to get a foothold on the steps. They were narrow and slick with ice, and the wind certainly didn't help matters, but eventually he was able to find his footing on them and begin to climb.

The staircase stretched on interminably, especially with how slow his progress was. He had to be careful with every single step, or else risk slipping and plummeting to the ground that soon vanished in the gale. He counted the steps as he went to keep himself focused.

"One hundred...two hundred...three hundred," and on and on. Ignoring the fact that his skin and clothes were covered with a layer of ice and his back and shoulders were piled with snow, he labored on. After a while he noticed that the winds were lessening and the sky above was changing shade ever so slightly the higher he went. Then, to his surprise, the clouds broke apart entirely, revealing a brilliant, ice-blue sky unmarred by the wintry storm. A few steps higher, he was able to look out over the top of the great cloud bank he had climbed out of, and also up the stairway to his destination.

His breath caught in his throat when he looked up the long narrowing ridge of black stone he was ascending. Like a huge blade it rose up out of the clouds, growing narrower and steeper with every step. At the very top, he could see that it was only a few inches wide, the steps so tall, it was almost a ladder. The polished black sides of the staircase fell off a sheer thousand feet, and he guessed that even with the snow's cushioning, his chances of surviving such a fall were slim to none. Though he had felt some fear of falling on the slick stone steps while in the clouds, he had not endured the true scale of the fall. He took a deep, shaky breath.

"These are just stairs," he said to himself. "Just regular stairs. I'm not going to fall down a regular flight of stairs."

The top of the blade of stone steps opened out onto a great crag of gray basalt which crowned a flat-topped mountain thrusting up from the swirling fog beneath, so steep-sided as to be approachable only by the staircase, or with pitons, ropes, and more than a little bit of foolish bravery. Gritting his teeth against his fear and the vertigo of the great height, Michael took one step, breathed deeply, then took another, and another. The last steps were less than half a foot wide, forcing him to place one foot directly in front of the other as he climbed. He bent over and clambered with his hands as well, trembling as he took the last few steps. When at last he reached the top step, he was shaking and sweating, expecting at any moment that he would slip and fall, and fall, and fall. He leapt from that step to the plateau and immediately lay flat on his stomach and crawled away from the edge onto the cold, flat stone.

He closed his eyes and lay there for a minute until his breathing steadied. Finally, he was able to sit up and look around, thrilled to be free of that accursed staircase. Though the air was still thin and cold, the sun overhead was strong enough to melt away much of the frost that had accumulated on him during the climb. He heard something squeaking softly and turned to see a metal sign hanging in a stand-rack, swinging just a little in a gentle breeze. Painted and lettered exactly like the signs at City of Rocks, it read, "Welcome to Pony Hill Recreational Revelation Park." To his great dismay, behind the sign stood a tall white door with a brass doorknob, exactly like the one he had seen in the intersection of the desert roads. What if it just took him right back where he came from? What if all of that had been for nothing? Then again, he certainly wouldn't mind being back with Ace and her trusty vehicle. It was a hell of a lot better than being stranded all alone on a frigid mountaintop.

Michael sat before the second white door on top of the black mountain for a very long time. He did not open or touch it. He surveyed the landscape and there seemed to be nowhere else to go, but still he waited. He definitely wasn't about to climb back down the staircase into the blizzard. He just sat on the cold stone in the icy clear air and waited for an idea to come to him.

Eventually, he could postpone the inevitable no longer. He stood and approached the door. But before he could touch it, the white door swung open of its own accord. Michael stepped back, ready for anything. From the darkness beyond the doorway, a tall Striker stepped out into the light, dressed in a long black robe and a baggy black hood. Michael looked about wildly for any route of escape, but the only one which presented itself was the lip of the cliff.

The Striker laughed and waved a hand. "Hey, take it easy, take it easy. I'm not who you think I am."

"Then who are you?" Michael said, suspicious.

"My name is Sebastian. I'm the spirit of the mountain here."

"What do you want with me?" Michael took a step backwards, still tense and ready for a fight.

"Don't be afraid of me, Spirit Man. I have come all the way up here to the top of the world overlooking all the kingdoms of Shook, just so I can teach you about the ways of the world and the secrets of the human heart. I figured you'd forgotten a lot of it." He gave a harsh chuckle at his own joke. "Come, follow me."

The spirit of the mountain walked past Spirit Man, to the far edge of the mountain, and sat down inside a small circle of white stones. Michael followed cautiously and sat down across from him, trying not to notice the abyss only a few feet away. With a deep sigh, the Striker reached up and took off his entire face, as if it were only a mask. He set the face aside, revealing beneath it the face of a compassionate monk.

"Is that better?" he said. "Now, we don't have much time and I have a lot of material to cover. Let me teach you about the ways of the world and the secrets of the human heart."

Michael still didn't know whether to trust this strange man. After all, things were rarely as they appeared in this world. Who could say if this face was the man's real face, or if Sebastian was his real name? What if it was all a ploy?

"Well," Michael said, "where do we start?"

"Tell me, son, what ails your heart?"

Michael's hand went instinctively to the slab of stone that had once been his chest. "It's complicated," he said.

"Most things are," said Sebastian. "But come, let me show you the way."

Hesitantly, Michael moved a little closer. Sebastian reached out his hand and touched the rough rock directly above the place where Michael's heart ought to have been. As he did so, something peculiar happened. It was like he was transmitting something, or giving something, but it was neither visible nor audible—it was, in fact, utterly undetectable to any of Michael's senses. Yet he detected it all the same. Something crossed from one man to the other, something important, only he had no idea what it was and felt no different when Sebastian removed his hand.

"What did you do?" Michael said.

Sebastian only smiled. "Okay, Spirit Man, that's all of it," he said. "You go ahead and take the door back now."

Michael sensed that he wouldn't get anything out of the man if he asked any questions. He stood to leave, shook Sebastian's hand, and then walked directly to the door. Without hesitation this time, he opened it and stepped right through.

He immediately found himself precisely in the intersection where he had just been, and the door winked out of existence behind him. And there, in front of him, sat the Hummer. Michael took a big breath, so relieved to find himself back with Ace. He wanted to tell her everything about what had just transpired, but at the same time felt the strange urge to tell her none of it at all. It had been such a private moment, really, hidden even from his conscious brain. It seemed wrong, in a way, to share it so crassly with someone else.

He found Ace asleep in the driver's seat and wondered just how long he had been gone. The Hummer's doors were locked, so he knocked gently on the door to wake her. She startled awake and, after a moment of surprise, smiled broadly at him.

"You're back!" she said, before quickly containing her excitement. "I mean. Good."

"Yes," Michael teased, "good indeed."

She stretched in her seat and gave a deep groan of satisfaction. "I thought you might come right back here," she said. "Figured I'd get a bit of shuteye while I waited."

Then she turned the key in the ignition and her trusty pal the Lemon Pie rumbled to life once more. She glanced again at Michael and shook her head, chuckling to herself.

"What?" he said.

"Nothing."

"No, what?"

"I'll tell you later," she said.

And they drove together into the vast expanse of the desert.

From the top of the great stone mountain, Sebastian watched the Hummer cruise across the barren red desert. He shook his head, then reached up and took off his monk's face. Beneath it was a golden mask, hiding the true face of Lord Striker. His jet-black robe slowly turned back into a deep royal blue. Beneath the mask, his face contorted into a strange kind of sorrow as he studied that yellow speck in the distance. He shook it off quickly, rolled his enormous shoulders, and disappeared through a door etched with black runes.

Chapter 10

The storm began innocently enough. The sky darkened on the horizon ahead of them, the air took on the smell of approaching weather. Michael had been taking advantage of the long drive to try to relax, allowing himself to doze now and then as he and Ace soared through the desert at breakneck speeds. They were racing well over a hundred miles an hour, Michael guessed, but they hadn't seen any speed limit signs, so he had to presume that Ace knew what she was doing. He leaned back against the firm padded seat of the Jeep and listened idly to the thrum of the rugged tires on the endless desert highway. In spite of their reckless speed, Michael felt at peace for the moment, enjoying this restful, calm pocket in the stress of his usual travels. Ace, too, seemed at peace, her goggles on, one hand on the wheel and the other out the window, resting against the side of the car.

Looking at Ace, Michael wanted to tell her how grateful he was for her. Not just for picking him up in the desert when he would have been walking for who knew how long, and not just for helping him on his journey, wherever it was taking him. He wanted to thank her for this feeling of peace, for making him feel like he didn't have to act like he knew exactly what was going to happen. For the first time in his many travels, Spirit Man felt like his work was actually being shared, like he didn't have to be the only one to bear the burden. Did she even realize how much she was helping him, how long he'd traveled and never had anyone make him feel so supported? Or was he really just like any other passenger to her, another lost soul in need of a helping hand?

His reverie was rudely interrupted by a sudden knife-edged rush of sound as a bolt of lightning struck the ground only a few feet from the side of the car, followed immediately by a teeth-rattling clap of thunder. Michael shouted in alarm and would have jumped out of his seat if it weren't for his seatbelt. That bolt was quickly followed by another, which landed on the other side of the road and missed the Hummer by inches.

Ace grabbed the steering wheel with both hands. "Shitfire," she said, "hold on, we'll be fine." She struggled to keep the vehicle straight on the road as a tremendous gust of wind slammed into their right side.

Michael was astonished to see how quickly the storm on the horizon had rolled over them. The entire sky was filled with roiling clouds of every shade of black, and among them flashed bolts of blue lightning. Another blinding blue bolt blasted down to the earth beside them, and then another. Seconds later, sheets of rain whipped across their windshield, driven by an angry, howling wind. Ace flipped on the windshield wipers, but it was like trying to wipe away the roaring whitewater to try to see the riverbed. She swore and let off the gas, allowing the Hummer to slow to a more controllable speed. The rain only pounded harder, big fat droplets crashing with such force they drowned out even the sound of the thunder.

"We've got to pull over!" shouted Michael, though he wasn't sure if Ace heard. He peered through the rain, trying to see anything of the landscape around them or the road ahead, but it was all a gray-blue blur.

"Don't worry, Michael, just stay calm," Ace yelled. "Storms here only last for a little while, and then they go away just as fast as they came along in the first place. We just gotta ride this out and it'll be like it never happened."

"Are you sure we should keep going?" They were still moving considerably faster than Michael was comfortable with, given the conditions. If there were any obstacles in the road, there was no way they'd see them before it was too late.

"Stop worrying!" she shouted back. "We're going to come up to Exit 115 soon, and my house is just off the exit there. We can get inside and get dry and it'll all be just fine."

Despite her apparent confidence, her knuckles were white as

she wrapped them around the steering wheel. Was she really so confident they'd make it, or was she just trying to make him feel better? Michael decided not to question it too much and just shut his mouth in a grim line, watching the road as if there was something he could do to stop the rain in front of them.

The thundering sky hurled down lightning bolts all around them, from horizon to horizon, striking things that Michael couldn't see through the distances and the rain. Bizarrely, most of them seemed to flash in a coordinated pattern, forming lines in the distance which drew nearer with each successive burst. It was almost as if a huge beasts with electricity for legs were advancing on them, marching ever closer to their vehicle. Soon, the dozens of crackling blue bolts became hundreds, ripping the sky with their constant booming and roaring.

Then Michael saw something even more astonishing than the army of marching lightning bolts. Every time a bolt touched down on the earth close enough for him to see, there stood a gold-masked Striker. They stepped out of the bursts of light as though it were some kind of magic elevator that had transported them from some terrible world in the sky. At first Michael thought he was imagining things, simply seeing things in the sheets of rain. But when he pointed them out to Ace, she bit her lip and cursed.

"I should've known," she said.

Unlike the bikers, each of these Strikers wore a royal blue double-breasted military uniform decorated with brass buttons. Each also sported a cape with the hood thrown back, exposing the masked faces to the wind and rain. For a moment, the rain parted and Michael saw before them an entire horde of Strikers. They marched like an army of leering corpses, their movements not quite right, not quite human, advancing on their singular target. Holding his head out into the rain so he could see around the flooded windshield, Michael could see the wild flaring eyes of the manic Strikers. Row upon row on them flanked the road on every side. There was no way out. The Strikers reached around behind them and all as one brought out their strange weapons. Each held a huge and unwieldy blunderbuss with brass trim and a bright-painted stock. With the wind whipping their hair and their capes, they all took aim and fired.

Michael flinched, expecting to feel the hot sting of the bullets, but instead nothing seemed to happen. He looked again and saw that from the barrel of each gun had popped a large flag on a stick, and each flag had a letter. All seen in a row, they read:

"THIS IS HELL AND ALL OUR FRIENDS ARE HERE."

"All right, you bastards are asking for it," Ace snarled into the wind. She pulled open a panel in the roof, letting in the whipping rain. Then she reached down beside her seat and pulled out a big leather purse, from which she drew a tiny bright red pistol. "Get in the driver's seat, Michael," she snapped.

"What?" he yelled. He must have misheard her in the rain. What was she planning? She grabbed his hands and wrapped his fingers around the wheel, patting his knuckles almost tenderly. Then she stood up in her seat and stepped easily over to Michael's seat, balancing herself with a hand on the open roof. Michael yelled as the car jerked, and he scrambled to slide into the driver's seat and steady them out.

"Ace, you're crazy!" he shouted, laughing in spite of himself.

Ace looked down at him and grinned, a broad smile that showed off her white teeth. Her goggles were still on, and her hair whipped in the manic winds of the storm. She looked like nothing less than a goddess of destruction.

"You don't know the half of it, sweetheart!"

Then she faced the road and began to blast away at the Strikers with deadly aim. The explosions from the little pistol were as loud as the thunderclaps, booming like an artillery cannon firing. The little red gat spat and spat. Each bullet she fired blasted the head right off one of the leering Strikers. In a few short seconds, she killed ten, twenty, thirty of the ugly buggers. The pistol appeared to have an infinite supply of whatever supercharged bullets it was using.

"Who the hell do you think you are?" Ace shouted over the roar of the storm and the jarring blasts of her pistol. "Who the hell you think you're dealing with, you wormy scum? I don't go down easy!" She gave a wild laugh and kept firing. How many rounds could that tiny little powerhouse of a gun hold?

Michael had to resist the urge to watch her do her deadly work as he drove the careening vehicle through the swirling winds. The rain had really done a number on the road, leaving it rutted with gullies and arroyos, and with puddles that hid suspension-wrecking chuckholes. Even the hardy Lemon Pie lurched and groaned when it hit them.

"Keep driving," Ace yelled at him. "Drive like your life depends on it!"

He did. He dropped down a gear and ran at higher engine rpm to give him a quicker response to the increasingly rutted and ragged road. He held the steering wheel tight, both his hands surging with determined strength, and began to aggressively press the big machine forward. Above him, Ace let out a whoop and a howl like a wild mountain wolf with the smell of blood in her nose, and began to fire faster and faster, matching the storm's intensity with the thunderous reports of her gun.

As Ace cut through their ranks, the remaining Strikers broke into a spring, clambering over their fallen comrades without so much as flinching and charging toward the gunfire as if they were utterly prepared to die. Michael didn't know exactly how many Strikers were out there, but he had long since lost count of how many times Ace had fired into the storm. Whenever he glanced away from the road, he saw piles of bleeding bodies, dead, dead, dead. But more Strikers were never far behind.

Ace suddenly stopped firing and pulled her head down into the inside of the truck. "Get ready to turn off to the right," she said. "Once we're off the highway, we'll lose 'em."

Seconds later, he saw what she was referring to. A huge green road sign big enough for an eight-lane highway dangled over the asphalt. "The One And Only Exit 115," it read. He had to jerk the wheel hard to make it. The car skidded and Ace swore as she tumbled into the passenger seat, but they made it—just barely.

Michael followed the exit ramp as it curved around a little hill, and continued onto the narrow road that waited beyond it. As soon as they rounded that bend, the rain stopped, as if someone somewhere had abruptly turned off the water valve. Seconds later, the sun came out from behind some scattered clouds, and the inside of the Hummer quickly dried out, as if it had never been drenched at all. Ace let out a long, low whistle and returned her gun to its hiding place. She ran her fingers through her hair as it began to dry in the sunlight.

"What did I tell you, Spirit Man?"

"Yeah, right, lucky guess, Spirit Woman." He wasn't sure where that had come from. It was sort of automatic, a reflex, and once he said it, it felt true.

"Spirit Woman," she said. A tiny smile tugged at the corner of her mouth. "Funny. I guess you're starting to catch on, then."

Michael glanced sideways at her, but before he could press her to elaborate, she pointed toward a mountain peak ahead of them.

"That's Torpedo Peak!" she said. "That's where we're going. Home's near there."

Michael put the Hummer into a lower gear and drove up a steep hill with cliffs of red clay on both sides, then eased down the other side which was, if anything, even steeper. He crossed over a dry creek bed identified by a small sign. He squinted to see what it would say and was a little disappointed when it read only "Stony Brook." Around a corner and onto a dusty road, he found himself bumping through a pleasant little valley with clusters of fat round trees. A closer look told him they were apple trees, though he wasn't sure how well those usually fared in a harsh desert climate like this one. He drove down the dirt road another hundred yards or so, then Ace signaled to him to make a right-hand turn onto her clean-swept, paved driveway.

Ace's home was a very small house made of tiny, rose-colored bricks, each a slightly different hue that made it almost seem covered in scales, like a fish. The two windows in the front were trimmed in light blue, and her front door was a deep blue. That made Michael a bit uncomfortable, but he put it quickly out of his mind as

Ace jumped from the vehicle and began to collect her things from the back, shaking off what remained of the rain.

She rolled her head back and forth and rubbed the back of her neck with a little groan. She tilted her head back and ruffled her hair, which had gotten significantly fluffier as it dried. Then she made a dramatic gesture toward the humble house.

"Home sweet home," she said proudly. "What do you think, Spirit Man?"

Once more, he noted that there was something absolutely captivating about the way she moved through the world, the little bursts of happiness and excitement which occasionally broke through her rough exterior. She might be nothing but a dream girl in a dream world, but Michael found himself wanting to believe in her, more than he'd ever felt like he could believe in anything. If he'd possessed his heart....But it wasn't worth dwelling on. They had bigger fish to fry.

"Beautiful," he said. "It's beautiful."

"C'mon, I'll give you the grand tour."

He grabbed an armful of her things and followed her to the door. Michael was surprised to find that she had not locked her door.

As if she could read his mind, she explained, "No one would dare mess with my house, so I keep it open. Strikers don't make it this far off the highway, and besides, even if they did, they know better than to mess with Ace's place." She winked. "And if they do show up, it'll be looking for little old you. But don't worry, I've got enough hidey holes and sniper spots around here that I think we'll be just fine."

Michael stepped through the front door, noticing as he did that the tiny bricks of her house were actually not bricks at all, but were in fact rose-colored dominos. He set her stuff down on the floor against the wall, and when he looked up again, Ace was considering him, her head tilted to one side.

"Everything okay?" she said, her voice gentle but inscrutable.

"Yeah, absolutely," Michael said. "I think?" He hadn't thought of himself as being anything other than okay, but clearly she was seeing something he wasn't. Was he okay? Or was it all becoming too much? The sensation that he should be whole, that he should be able to feel, to really feel in this moment.

"I see," she said. "You're just completely blown away by my decorating skills." She swept a hand out dramatically to take in the house. "Or you simply cannot fathom the depths of my hospitality." She fluttered her eyelashes in an exaggerated manner.

"That's exactly it," he said. "You've got me all figured out."

"Oh, more than you know." She grinned. "Anyway, how about that grand tour? Special show, one time only offer."

Ace took him by the hand and together they walked in a tight circle around the living room. It was very small, with a short little couch on one side and two straight wooden chairs beside a card table on the other. An opening without a door led to a little kitchen on one side, and a tiny hallway led to a pair of doors on the other. Though very plain, it was homey and comfortable. She led him to the card table, and his attention was caught by a framed photograph hanging on the wall above it. It was a picture of Ace, but the photograph was clearly old, the whole thing cast in a faded sepia. She was holding a tennis racket, and wearing the polo shirt, tennis skirt, and saddle shoes of a 1940s tennis outfit. Behind her extended a railing, and several rows of bench seats, like pews, overlooking a bay, and a cluster of smokestacks. "That's the Catalina Island ferry," he said, surprised he recognized it, "about 1941."

"Don't be silly," she said. "That's just down the street." She pointed to the chessboard set up on the table. "Take a look at that and tell me what you think. It's something I've been pondering over for a while, and I'm curious to hear your thoughts."

"Sure," he said. He examined the board, where a game was already in progress. He had played more than a few games with the janitor John Lohman once upon a time, and Lohman had taught him a few quick and dirty chess plays. Looking at this board, however, Michael could only tell that the board was well-balanced. Neither side had an advantage. The only thing about the game that really stood out was that there was only one Queen on the board, and she was neither black nor white, but royal blue.

　　　　　　　　　　HEART OF THE SPIRIT MAN

"All right, how about a clue here," he said, pointing to the blue Queen. "Who is she?"

"You know exactly who she is," Ace said. "And so does she. Look, here's how it works. Either player can use the Queen. The only rule is that if I move the Queen, we both must make one move with another piece before you can move the Queen—and then vice versa."

"What about capturing her?" he asked.

"Don't be silly," she laughed. "Why would you want to take your own Queen?" But she watched him closely, as if she was recording his answers in some part of her mind so she could read over them later.

"She makes the game almost meaningless, don't you think?" he asked. "She's going to slaughter half the pieces on both sides, and no matter which side loses, she wins. It's her game more than anyone else's."

"Maybe. The Queen is truly the most powerful piece in her universe," Ace said, "but she is not more powerful than the player." She tilted her head at him and he got that sense again that she was measuring him up, taking stock of him.

"That's poor consolation when she takes out my Knight," he said.

"When you move a Knight, are you a Knight? When a Knight falls, do you? Just some food for thought, Spirit Man. Come on, we'll play this game out later. I think it's fine on its own for now."

Michael frowned but followed her. He didn't get the sense she had planned on really letting him play the board, and he felt like a scholar, trying to puzzle out the meaning of an ancient text.

Ace led him to the little hallway, and to the two doors. One was slightly open, and he could see the end of an old-fashioned lion-footed iron bathtub within. The other, closed, was the most breathtaking shade of blue, marked in the gold letters of a star's dressing room, which spelled out: "ACE'S DREAMING PLACE." The door creaked as it swung wide open. Michael had to lean to one side to peek into the darkened space. There was just enough light to see the room was completely empty except for an ornate 19th-century psychiatrist's couch, upholstered in royal blue with blood-red brocade. If there were any windows behind any of the floor-to-ceiling drapes, they were not admitting a drop of light. With the door shut, Michael imagined it would be pitch black.

"This is what I needed to find here," he said, somehow knowing intuitively that this was true. He turned to ask Ace a question, but the words died on his lips. Her eyes were closed and her hands were pressed over her heart. She lowered her chin and allowed her hair to hang around her face, nearly hiding her expression. She looked so solemn it struck a strange kind of fear into Michael. He half expected her to break her trance and make some kind of joke, or tease him for being gullible, but instead she began to murmur in a low, serious voice.

"Spirit Man," she said softly. He leaned closer to her to hear her better. "Go you now into the dreaming room, where spin the ever-twining threads of the worlds, the binds and ties of your mind. Go, Spirit of Man, go and seek silence and sound, seek vision and blindness. Let the worlds spin before you and pluck themselves from your sky. I command thee, Spirit Man, go you to learn what you can from the hearth of Spirit Woman, where dreams are bred and born and live and die. Learn what you can to recover the heart of Michael Seymour. And ponder this question, Spirit Man: When you rise from a dream, do all those you met in the dream awaken?"

A tear slid down one cheek as she finished her chant with a tiny gasp, almost of pain. Then she slumped back against the wall and took a heavy breath, finally opening her eyes to blink up at him. Tears glimmered in her dark eyes, and she gestured to the room with a nod.

Without more hesitation than it took to give her a sign of grateful acknowledgment, and without a word, he walked past her and into her room of dreams and visions.

The old door creaked once again as she shut it, leaving Spirit Man all by himself in total darkness. He groped around the tiny room, knees bent like a man newly blind. Then he stopped, took control of himself, and reminded himself that he had seen the room, and knew exactly where the couch was located and that nothing else had been in the room. He chided himself for fearing that obstacles had been placed in his path as soon as the light was gone, and he took two steps, turned around, and sat down—exactly on the middle of the little lounge bed.

He lay down on the bed on his back, folded his hands over his chest, and tried to stare up at the ceiling. All he could see was the usual purple and green display of his retina fatigue. He rubbed his eyes to make the colors flash and move, but he knew he was seeing nothing. He took a deep breath, sighed, then closed his eyes and allowed himself to drift into sleep. He slipped back beneath the waves, into a deep, dark dream.

In Michael's dream, he saw Lord Striker, the stormy god, wearing a black hood tightly wrapped around his head, his gold-masked face barely visible in the darkness within. A gust of wind blew across the universe and Michael heard Striker cry out, "I am sorry for what I have done! I am sorry! Will you ever forgive me?"

Michael felt his spirit leave his body to soar through dark skies brimming with millions upon millions of stars, until Spirit Man stood before Lord Striker Himself. Michael's spirit then asked the god of Shook, "Why is there so much suffering in the world? Why must we all die? And why do you perpetuate these awful things?"

Lord Striker turned his dark visage upon Spirit Man and said, "You might as well ask why there is sunset and night."

"You mean that there can't be light without darkness?" Spirit Man said.

"No," said Striker, shaking his head. "Here is the answer to your questions: The sun is always shining."

Spirit Man's feet gave out from underneath him and he cried out as he fell into darkness, his body spinning out of control. He fell backwards through space and time, through a landscape of darkness and shadows, down, down, down, and back to Ace's room.

He woke up with a gasp and found himself staring into the dark. He tried to steady his ragged breathing and frantically rubbed the sleep from his eyes with the heels of his hands. He fumbled to stand and as he reached out in the darkness, the door swung open and let in light. Michael winced, the brightness stinging his eyes, and fell back on the couch.

"Morning, Spirit Man," a soft voice said.

Michael squinted to see Ace standing in the doorway, leaning against it. He remembered now, coming into the room, lying down to sleep. The look on Ace's face when she opened the door, the tear running down her cheek.

He stood up and went to her, putting his hands on her shoulders and peering into her eyes.

"Are you all right?" he asked, searching her face.

She looked back up at him and tilted her head, smiling softly.

"A fine hello to you, too."

Michael dropped his hands and rubbed the back of his neck. "Sorry. Good morning. Only...Last night, you looked..."

She gave a little scoff of a laugh and smiled up at him. "You're sweet to worry. I'm only sorry I couldn't give you better warning." She looked past him to the couch. "I...We all have our roles to play, I guess. You know, in a dream, how you do things because they feel right, not because they make sense?"

He nodded.

"That's all." She shrugged and headed toward the kitchen. "Come on, Spirit Man, dreams are over. We gotta eat now."

The table in the kitchen was set with the sort of meager, stable fare of someone who doesn't spend a lot of time at home. There were bowls of oatmeal, apple chips, saltine crackers with jelly spread, and canned beans warmed up over the stove. A pot of coffee was starting to whistle and Ace took it off the burner, setting it on an oven mitt beside jars of sugar and powdered creamer. "Sorry it's not much," she said. "I don't keep things here that spoil, since I'm gone so often."

"It looks great," he said, sitting down across from her.

They each took their fill and began to eat in silence, the weight of the dream room hanging between them. Michael couldn't stop thinking of how she'd looked before sending him in, her hands clasped over her chest, her voice so soft and unlike herself. Neither could he stop thinking of how different Lord Striker had been in his dream. Not the wicked, boastful, taunting face he had known, but wounded somehow, incomplete.

After a long silence, broken only by the sounds of spoons scraping against bowls and muted chewing, Ace said, "All right, here's my plan. After breakfast, we'll head out to the border of the two worlds. I know the way and I can get you there in time. I don't have it all figured out yet, what I'll be able to do to help you, but I can at least get you to the border. After that, you'll be on your own. Understand?"

He nodded. "Yeah, I do." He'd only been traveling with her for about two days, and yet he hated the thought of going on to Lord Striker's lair without her. Why couldn't she come? Then again, perhaps it was for the best. If Lord Striker could inflict the Second Death on someone, a permanent end, the last person Michael wanted in the room with that madman was Ace.

"So tell me," he said, "what will I find at this border?"

"That's all going to be up to you to find out, Spirit Man," she said, downing the last of her coffee. "I'm afraid I don't have nearly as many answers as I would like. All I know is it'll get you one step closer to where you need to be."

Michael looked around her little home, filled with warmth and subtle pieces of her. He didn't want to leave. On the kitchen shelf, she had a model of a tiny coliseum, the sort of odd knick-knack she might have picked up on her travels. Its walls were painted blood red. On the kitchen counter among the dirty dishes sat a teacup, glinting with a fake gold polish, fallen over on its side. A painting of a huge, starry tower that stretched into the dark clouds around it hung over the sink and bore the signature "ACE" in the left corner. Everything about the place seemed familiar somehow, intriguing in a way he couldn't quite put his finger on. All he wanted was to stay until he'd learned it all, until he knew everything about this unusual woman. He wanted to learn her language.

But he finished his breakfast, wiped his mouth with the back of his hand, and said, "I think I'm ready."

Ace smiled at him a little sadly. "I think you are, too," she said. They packed up the Hummer and set out again on the highway.

Chapter 11

Night fell upon the dream world like a door slamming shut. Ace and Michael were back on the highway, cutting across the barren Wastelands of Shook at breakneck speeds. The pavement was smooth and black as a frozen lake at midnight, and it was much narrower than the highway they had previously driven, with barely enough room for the Lemon Pie to fit. Ace chewed on her lip as she drove. The glare from the high beams reflected off her goggles, making her appear otherworldly, futuristic, like someone out of a neo-noir science fiction film that didn't end well for its heroes. The Hummer's deep growling engine and the whipping wind around it were the only sounds in the universe. Michael wondered, a little bittersweet, if he'd ever get used to Ace's crazy speed behind the wheel. He hoped he would have enough time to get used to it, but knew that their journey was barreling toward its conclusion.

The narrowness of the road made him especially nervous about other cars. The idea of trying to navigate around another car approaching from the opposite direction was one he didn't much want to entertain. Of course, besides the Strikers, they actually hadn't seen other vehicles on the road at all. Friendly—or even neutral—faces were few and far between in these parts. In his other adventures, there had always been people out and about, living their strange lives. But here, in this place under Lord Striker's dominion, it seemed the only beings allowed to roam freely were the vicious armies of that cruel lord. It resulted in the feeling that the entire world existed just for him and Ace, an open desert road with nothing to distract from the wind and the journey. In a strange way, he was almost glad that they hadn't seen anyone else. He didn't want them to see the famous Spirit Man like this, without a heart and turning to stone. Who would they look up to then? Who would they trust to save them?

As they drove through the dark night, the ruins of an old fort appeared alongside the road ahead of them. Ace glanced at it, but gave no reaction at all, as though it were just another long-abandoned, crumbling shack. The old fort appeared to have been in a terrible war a long time ago. Most of the battle-scarred walls were falling, and huge holes gaped here and there, as if they'd been blown apart by cannon blasts. The lookout tower was badly charred and appeared that it might collapse at any moment, In fact, it seemed impossible that it was still standing at all. It swayed precariously back and forth in the windless night.

The whole fort, bizarrely, was lighted by a row of pale yellow streetlamps, the only lights he had seen all night. But who were these lights for? There were no signs of anybody around, nor of any business offering services to passersby. He considered for a moment asking Ace to pull off the highway so they could get a better look, but no exits presented themselves, and he figured it was best not to waste any more time.

As they drew closer to the fort, nearly overtaking it, Michael jolted in his seat at the realization that he recognized the place. It was Fort Huachuca, he realized, the name coming slowly back to his mind as he recalled the strange times he'd had there, partying and getting drunk and shooting the piss with Emmitt del Rio and the rest of his diminutive cavalry, thirsty in the Badlands of Chaos. What on earth was the fort doing here? It looked as if it had been abandoned to the wastes of time, ravaged by years and wars, with none of the vivacity, none of the life he remembered.

He started to ask Ace if she knew how far they were from the Badlands of Chaos, or if in fact she knew of that place at all, but her apparent indifference to the fort made him hold back. Maybe it wasn't the same fort after all. It did look different in the off-kilter light of those lamps. Maybe he only wanted it to be Fort Huachuca out of desperation for something familiar amid all this strangeness and uncertainty. Better to keep quiet, for now, and maybe ask later if he could determine with surety that it really was Fort Huachuca.

   HEART OF THE SPIRIT MAN

The Hummer hit a bump, hard, and then another. Without warning, the smooth road became rough and shoddy, ridden with potholes, chunks of broken pavement, and patches of gravel and sand. Ace had to wrestle with the wheel to control the vehicle, as the terrain challenged even her trusty steed. Soon the pavement was gone altogether and they bounced and jostled along a pitted dirt road in dire need of maintenance.

"What happened?" Michael said. "It looks like we've run out of road."

"That's because we're almost there," she said, pointing ahead. Out of the darkness loomed a huge gray steel tower. Michael gulped looking up at it, its foreboding walls, so high it seemed it might breach the atmosphere. He couldn't help but wonder if this was the place that had so wrecked the fort they had passed. He could easily picture fireballs and cannons blasting from the sides of that ominous tower.

Ace pulled up right next to it and stopped. With its base embedded in a huge cement platform, the steel tower looked as sturdy as any skyscraper as it soared straight up into the dark night, disappearing into shadow above them. It seemed impossibly tall, taller than any building Michael had ever seen. It was as if he was looking at a gray piece of the sky itself, stretching up into space forever.

"What is this place?" Michael said, leaning back as far as he could to peer up toward the top. He still couldn't see anything that might indicate the tower's purpose.

"We're at DW #15 Main Station," she told him as she turned off the engine. She put her hands inside the pockets of her blue jean jacket and settled down into her seat with a little sigh. They'd been driving all day, no stops, nothing but a sandwich several hours ago to sate their hunger. She pulled her goggles up to rest on her head and he saw how exhausted she was. She took a pull of water from her bottle.

"What are we looking for here? What do we do now?"

"We wait, Spirit Man," she said. She handed him the bottle of water and fished the paper bag where she'd packed some food from the backseat. "Eat if you need it. I'm going to get some rest, and you should, too. Get your strength up."

"Do I even get a hint about what to expect?"

"Come on, where would be the fun in that?" She flashed him a little smile, then leaned her seat back and settled deeper down into it. She shut her eyes, took two long, slow, deep breaths, and fell fast asleep as if she'd pressed a button. Michael studied her for a moment, listening to her breathing in the quiet of the night. Her hair splayed messily across the headrest and her arms were curled around her stomach as if she was keeping her guts from spilling out. To look at her in a moment like this, a moment of vulnerability, one might never guess that not twenty-four hours ago she had been unleashing unimaginable death and violence against Lord Striker's fanatical followers. Then again, hadn't Spirit Man done the same in the Badlands of Chaos? They were alike in that way—humble exteriors hiding immense potential for bloodshed. But was it right to put her in situations where she was forced to kill? Had he done the right thing when he had first flagged down her car?

No use thinking too much about that now. They had come this far together, and he had a feeling that if he told Ace to leave him before she was good and ready, he'd get a punch in the gut for his trouble. She was not one to be told what to do.

He tucked himself into the corner of his own seat and allowed old memories to resurface as he drifted toward sleep. He was in his bedroom listening to his extensive CD collection. Bob Dylan was whining and creaking a song about the darkest hour always being right before the dawn, and his parents knocked on the door and spilled into the room with no faces. When had he forgotten their faces? He had thought he never would.

What seemed like only seconds later, Ace sat bolt upright, jolting Michael back to wakefulness.

"What time is it?" she said. When Michael didn't answer right away, still a little groggy, she punched his shoulder and shook him. "Get up, quick! Now!"

"What? What?" He pushed himself upright and rubbed his eyes

and looked around, trying to search out the threat. He saw nothing, no approaching armies, no menacing visage of Lord Striker.

"We've got to get you going," she said. "I overslept, and now we're late, damn me! You better hope we don't miss the next train for you, sweetheart. We gotta go, let's get moving!"

Ace jumped out of the car and began sprinting across the dirt field toward the steel tower, barely taking the time to grab her keys. Michael roused himself and ran after her, still feeling foggy with sleep. When they arrived at the base of the tower, he saw a flight of steep stairs leading up into the night, curling around the tower in a spiral. Without slowing down, Ace ran up the stairs, taking them two at a time, and Michael followed. They dashed up five flights, then ten, then more. Michael expected to get tired at any moment, but it was as if friction and gravity hardly applied to him on this staircase. He soon found himself taking the stairs five, ten, twenty at a time, zipping up the tower like he was flying. Below, the ground shrunk into nearly nothing, the Lemon Pie becoming a dot, a speck, and then disappearing into the desert surrounding it. The air got colder and wetter as he climbed, and still he wasn't out of energy. Nor was Ace, flying just ahead of him, every bit as untiring as he was.

When they finally reached the top level, they found a small platform lit by a single pale yellow bulb, which illuminated a sign that read "DW #15 Main Station," just as Ace had said. Ace walked along a yellow painted railing and then toward a long line of monorail cars which sat in dark silence on a single track. When they got within a few feet of the first monorail car, bright lights inside automatically turned on, flooding the entire area with light. Two doors then slid open, making way for the incoming passengers.

"Come on, slowpoke," Ace said. She grabbed his hand and pulled him into the monorail car with her. "There," she said, a little smug with satisfaction. "Told you we'd make it. And you were worried!"

The doors hissed shut behind them and the lights dimmed to a comfortable level.

"But seriously," she said. "That sure was close." She shivered in the chill of the thin air and sat down on one of the seats. Michael sat beside her. She didn't drop his hand, and he didn't let go of hers.

"Was it?" he asked. "Looked to me like this thing has been here waiting for us for years."

"Well, of course it has," she said, "but if we hadn't gotten here when we did, we would have missed it. It never would have left."

As he pondered the logic of that, an electronic bell sounded, followed by a deep voice which spoke with all the weariness and flatness of tone of a senior-citizens' tour bus guide.

"Welcome to the DW Main Train, where we maintain the main-frame, retain the main game, and you gain the fast lane. Enjoy your trip. It may be the last one you ever take." The voice then rumbled in deep-throated laughter and faded away in a series of distant echoes.

"That doesn't sound especially promising," Michael said.

"Oh, don't worry about it. It's a figure of speech."

With a series of quick bumps and jolts, the train lurched into motion. As they left the station, Michael saw a single tall pole rising up from the darkness below, supporting a sign. Just legible in the light of a pale yellow bulb was its message: "Dreams come and go. It is up to you to catch them."

The monorail car glided faster and faster along its narrow track. Shooting stars flared across the dark skies around them, creating a distant sort of light show. At a certain point, he lost track of whether they were continuing to accelerate or just moving at a steady, blindingly-fast rate. Was it possible for a train to break the sound barrier?

"Where are we going, Ace?" Michael said.

But she didn't answer him as they zoomed along through the darkness and deep silence of the sky. Instead, she only squeezed his hand and tried to hide the slightly worried expression that had etched itself across her face.

They arrived at the next stop, DW #17 Station, about fifteen min-utes later. The monorail car pulled into the tiny station at the end of its line. With a bump and a jolt, the car hit a thick rubber stop-per at the end of the tracks. Ace sat up in her hard plastic seat and

Michael did the same, still holding onto her hand for some kind of reassurance.

"What do we do now?" he said. Her hand in his made him feel simultaneously stronger and more afraid. She made him feel supported, braver, but he was acutely aware of what he was likely to lose as he continued forward with his journey.

"We keep going," Ace said. "This is our stop."

They stood and waited for the two sliding doors to open up. Once they did, the two of them then stepped out onto the crumbling concrete platform. There was only one pale yellow streetlight at the tiny station, which barely lit the area in front of them. The whole station was badly run down and completely empty. Who had built it, and for what purpose? Could it really just be there for them, for this one arrival?

"Sure is quiet out here," Michael said. The light overhead flickered eerily. Ace let go of his hand and he looked to see her frowning, biting her lips with worry. *She is scared to be here*, he realized. Very scared. And that terrified him.

The quiet made way for the sound of footsteps approaching rapidly, running toward them. As the heavy footfalls drew nearer, Michael tried to count them, but there were far too many. He saw Ace pat her pockets, searching for her gun, and come up empty.

"Shit," she said. "Shit, I left it in the car."

Then Michael saw something he had hoped he would never see again: a large battalion of Strikers rushing toward them at full speed. They were all dressed in their royal blue uniforms and wielded beautifully polished rifles and swords. Michael looked for a way out and found none. The monorail doors were closed and the station had only one door. The Strikers spilled through the dark doorway of the tiny station and onto the cement platform where Michael and Ace stood. They quickly surrounded the pair and leveled their guns at their heads and their swords at their chests. Just when Michael expected them to open fire, they stopped and held position. They were waiting for someone.

Then, an unusually tall Striker stepped past the others. His uniform was bedecked in medals, and his gold mask had been polished to a shine. He strolled right up to Michael. Through the mask, Michael saw him smile, revealing teeth that had been filed down to points to mimic the dagger fangs of his god.

"Well," he said. "Look who's finally decided to show up. I was beginning to get tired of waiting. Make one funny move and you're both dead, understand? Understand?"

Michael nodded slowly.

"Good. Now let's go, Spirit Man."

Michael's instinct was to punch him right in his wretched jaw, but Ace gave a tiny shake of her head, as if she realized what he was thinking, and he held himself back, gritting his teeth. The Strikers moved closer and prodded Michael and Ace with their weapons, urging the two of them forward. They led the pair to the station office and herded them inside. The tall Striker sat in a wooden chair behind the desk and motioned for Michael and Ace to sit as well. When they refused, he made another gesture and his men pushed the two captives roughly into their seats.

"I should introduce myself," the tall Striker said. "I am Captain of Division 73, the division which just so happens to control this area. Welcome to enemy territory."

"Too afraid to give us your name?" Michael said.

The captain laughed. "You really are out of your element, aren't you, Spirit Man?" He motioned to the Strikers standing behind them, weapons still drawn and at the ready. "We have no names besides Striker. We give them up when we swear our undying loyalty to Lord Striker, and in their place, we take His name for our own. If you must refer to me by any name, you may simply call me by my rank. I've worked hard to earn it."

It was then that Michael realized one of the captain's eyes was white and blank. A scar ran across the flesh around it like a reminder of the strike that had rendered the eye blind. The captain made another motion with his right hand and a brightly-colored bird emerged from behind a stack of papers. It alighted on his shoulder and pecked affectionately at his long, curly black hair. A parrot, from the looks of it, though Michael had never quite learned the difference between the various types of tropical bird. What made it even harder to tell was that the bird had almost no feathers left at all. Its back and neck were roughly scabbed, and its scrawny body shook almost constantly. Michael found himself feeling sorry for the creature.

"So," rumbled the deep voice of the captain, "do you have anything to say for yourselves before my men here escort you to your certain demise?"

The parrot extended his long scrawny featherless neck and squawked, "Drop dead, One-Eye! Drop dead, One-Eye!"

Michael and Ace said nothing.

"Very well." The captain stood and drew a long silver sword from his belt. He leveled it at them and said, with an air of calm smugness, "Take them to the compound."

"Drop dead, One-Eye!" squawked the parrot.

Several soldiers grabbed Michael and Ace by their arms and legs and hoisted them fully into the air. Then they marched them across the cement platform of the tiny station at gunpoint. The situation wasn't looking great, Michael had to admit, but he was just glad they weren't being handcuffed. They might be able to do something, with their hands free like that. He just couldn't think of what that something might be yet. All the Strikers had their swords and rifles at the ready, and they took turns pointing the tips and barrels right up against the small of their captives' backs, cackling with enthusiasm. Ace remained stoic in the face of their taunts, and Michael tried his best to do the same.

The Strikers carried them outside the station and Michael was surprised to find that they were at ground level again, once more in the desert under the same starry night sky. The Striker soldiers marched them into a shanty town and through a small plaza which was completely deserted, except for a few drunken Strikers and a skinny black dog. The beast was panting as though it had been running all day, and it looked like it was starving to death. It tried begging for food from a pair of Strikers who were slurping down a stew of some kind, and in response, the Strikers started kicking the poor creature. Ace opened her mouth in fury, but clamped it shut again when one of the Strikers grinned at her and said, "Hey, hey, missy, every word an extra kick, eh?"

The soldiers marched the pair onto a street of cobblestones, where a line of beat-up green army trucks and jeeps were parked side by side. The captain stood to the side as they were carried to the trucks and leaned in close as they passed.

"The darkest hour may be right before the dawn," he said. "But that's a dawn you'll never see, so if I were you, I wouldn't hold my breath."

The soldiers laughed and took both of them to a big truck with a long flat bed in the back. Wooden railings encircled three sides of the bed truck, but it didn't have a gate in the back at all. The Strikers tossed Michael and Ace into the back of the flatbed truck like two sacks of fresh green chile to be roasted. Then they jumped up onto the bed with them. They sat down on wooden crates along the sides of the bed and kept their guns and swords aimed squarely at their captives.

The captain slapped the back of the truck, indicating it was ready to go, and strolled away.

"Drop dead, One-eye! Drop dead, One-eye!" the parrot screeched out over and over, still perched on the captain's shoulder. And over the parrot's cries, the captain belted out orders to his men. Just as the convoy began pulling away, he climbed into the passenger side of a green army jeep and took off with them.

With a great rumbling of tires and coughing of old engines, the caravan of trucks and jeeps kicked up huge clouds of dust and left the monorail station and the shanty town behind. One of the soldiers in the back of the truck took a cigarette out of his shirt pocket and lit it up. The Striker took a heavy drag from it and Michael watched the smoke curl up into a long and slender white snake. He followed the trail of white smoke drifting out of the back of the truck until it disappeared into the night. All he could think of was leaving bread-crumbs, something to help track them back to where they were supposed to be. He reached over to Ace and grasped her hand, and she squeezed back gently.

The night was hot and humid and it felt like it had just rained. They rode in the back of the truck for hours, eventually reaching another seemingly abandoned settlement, which a huge blue sign declared to be Old Shook City. The streets were cobblestone and the buildings looked like they'd come straight from a medieval English town. Most windows were boarded up and there wasn't a living soul around. Michael imagined most of the residents had already either fled Lord Striker's armies or else had been slaughtered by these brutes.

The caravan of army trucks and jeeps made a looping righthand turn off the cobblestone streets of Old Shook City and onto the soft white sands of South Gehenna Beach. Michael was glad to leave the city behind, in part because the whole place made him profoundly uneasy, and in part because bouncing off all those cobblestones had been a deeply unpleasant experience on the hard bed of that old truck.

To the truck's left, ocean waves pounded a long sandy shoreline. Bizarrely, the sight of a sea instilled a strange glimmer of hope swept within him. After so long in those dry, inhospitable places, even glimpsing the sea as a captive seemed like a good omen.

They rode along the beach for another hour or so before they turned once again, then slowed down to a snail's pace as they navigated between large dunes of red sand. Michael kept expecting the Strikers to lash out with kicks, but they seemed to be holding themselves back for some reason. The captain and his driver led the way, but occasionally fell back to check in on the captives. Eventually the convoy came upon a row of old buildings and tiny shacks made out of pieces of rotten wood and gray cinder blocks, nestled among the red dunes. The dreary settlement was lighted with a row of baleful blue streetlights. The captain's jeep eased to a stop before a row of old buildings and the rest of the caravan did the same.

The driver turned off the engine as the captain got out of his jeep and stepped onto the gravelly parking lot.

Taking a wide-spread stance, the captain shouted, "Don't just stand there, you slobbering goons. Put them in the jail house, lock them up, and throw away the keys! If they get away, some Striker heads are going to end up in the taco machine, you hear me? Now move it!"

The soldiers yanked Michael and Ace out of the truck and threw them to the ground. Others wrenched them roughly to their feet and dragged them across the parking lot while others held them at gunpoint. They clearly weren't about to take any chances with these particular fugitives. And above it all, the captain's parrot continued to screech, "Drop dead, One-Eye! Drop dead, One-Eye!"

One of the soldiers opened the door to the dank and crumbling jailhouse, and the other Strikers threw Michael and Ace into their cell and slammed the door shut behind them. It was very dark inside the cell, lit only by one small square window, which gave them a glimpse into the outside world that lay beyond. The night sky was full of distant galaxies and twinkling stars, and their faint light barely lit up the prison cell. It could hardly dispel the aura of gloom and doom but it did give Michael some comfort to think about the infinite number of other worlds out there. Worlds better than this one, he hoped, though he had to admit it was just as possible that they were worse, that the wretched things which defined this world were in fact necessities of anywhere that held intelligent life. He looked up at the thick steel bars that crisscrossed the small square window of their prison cell.

"I'm not sure we're going to get out of here," he said.

"It wasn't supposed to go this way," Ace mumbled. She sat heavily on the concrete floor and examined her hands in the dark as if she might find a map there, a crucial note written by some previous version of herself that she had forgotten.

Michael was out of ideas. He was out of strength, too, suddenly drained by the impossibility of their predicament. In the distance, gunshots popped across the night, met with the sound of drunken laughter from the captain's men. Celebrating their success, their great victory. And why not? Soon enough, someone would come to the cell and put an end to Michael and Ace both. He touched his left shoulder and found that the stone had begun spreading down his bicep. It extended now across his entire torso, left to right, and crept onto his right shoulder as well. His neck, too, was stone all the way up to his Adam's apple. He could feel the weight of it all pulling him down. How easy it would be to lie on this floor and, before long, become part of it. His thoughts were interrupted by Ace.

"Have I ever told you the story of the two prisoners?" she said.

"I don't think so. I don't remember."

"Well," she began. "There were two prisoners who shared the same cell, as small as this one. They had been there for many long and hard years, both serving life sentences with no chance of ever getting out of prison at all. It was night, dark as hell, just as it is here right now in this hole of ours. The two prisoners woke up exactly at the same time in the middle of the night, and they stood up together and they looked through the small window in their prison cell. The same view both had had for so very, very long. But tonight it was a little different, though both were still looking through the same window." She paused for a long time, and in the total silence, she looked out through the bars in the window of their own cell. "Do you know what the two prisoners saw on that night through the bars of their tiny window?"

Michael shook his head.

"One saw mud," she said. "But the other one...the other one saw stars."

"Who told you that story?" Michael said.

"A friend of mine," she said, "a friend with a very bad reputation." As she stood looking up at the night sky, Ace seemed to be in some kind of trance. Michael too looked up at the night sky, and together they saw a universe of possibilities.

"Everything is going to be okay, Michael, you wait and see. You are going to get your heart back, I know you will. And dammit, I'll be there to help you."

He said nothing. He didn't want to break the spell. It was so pretty to think that what she said could ever be true.

Chapter 12

Michael awoke to piercing light. He shielded his eyes as he sat up and scrambled away from the jagged sunlight which cut through the bars. Morning had broken above the Sea of Gehenna, sunlight sparkling across the sand, glinting like millions of tiny mirrors and refracting into the air as if to heat the entire world. Michael rubbed his eyes, the events of the day before coming back to him slowly. He sat up and rubbed at the back of his sore neck, the portion which was not yet petrified stiff from a night sleeping on the floor. He'd been spoiled by the last few nights of sleep, on Ace's couch in the dreaming room, or under the stars in a sleeping bag with Ace beside him.

The quiet of the cell suddenly seemed huge. He heard only his own breathing, only the whispering of the sandy sea beyond the prison bars. He sat bolt upright in a way that sent a jolt of pain through his stiff back. Ace was no longer in the cell.

Fear shot through Michael like electricity. "Ace!" he cried, leaping to his feet and running to the door, listening hard. He could hear no one in the hall. In desperation, he ran back to the window, grabbing the bars as if he could pull them apart. There was nothing but sand and sun outside. "Ace, where are you?" Michael shouted. He paced back and forth in the cell, running a hand through his greasy hair.

He needed to think. They took her, but where? He didn't even know where he was, really, or what was around. He went back to the prison door, jiggling the handle hopelessly. To his shock, the door creaked open. Had they forgotten to lock it when they took her? Or was something else at play? He kept his hand on the handle and slowly swung the door open, peering down the hall both ways. No one was there, only a few candles guttering in sconces. He crept out into the hall, his blood pounding, straining to hear anything that might be coming. He couldn't let himself believe that he might be caught, or that Ace could already be...

He made it outside and ducked into an alleyway to avoid detection. Pressed against the wall of the jailhouse, however, he realized he couldn't hear anything but the wind. No voices, no screeching parrot. He emerged to find that all the jeeps and trucks were gone. The ramshackle stretch of buildings seemed completely abandoned. Tire tracks stretched across the sand, leading off into the dunes beyond. They had taken her with them, they must have, in the night. But why leave him? Wasn't he the main target? He stopped short. He was the target, right? Him, not Ace. He had to be. But something didn't add up, there was something he was missing, and now, because of that, Ace was in grave danger.

The wind howled across the dunes and the beach just out of sight, flinging up little dust clouds into the air. Michael had been alone through so many of his journeys in the past, but this was the first time he felt alone down to his very spirit. He'd been in pain, hopeless, furious, but never before had he felt as if even his own spirit had left him. Somewhere overhead, a seagull screeched and circled the blazing sun.

Michael couldn't get his thoughts in order, couldn't formulate a plan. He crossed the dunes and walked to the edge of the sea where the waves were gently rolling in and out in long sheets of white foam.

"Where do I go from here?" he cried out to the ocean, unsure of who he wanted to hear him, but knowing he needed to be heard. "What do I do?"

The ocean offered no reply but for the shush-shushing sound of the waves breaking lazily against the shore.

Michael walked back to the tire tracks by the jailhouse. With no other ideas, he might as well try following them, though he knew he had little hope of catching up with motorized vehicles on foot. But maybe wherever they had gone was close enough that he wouldn't die of thirst or starvation before he got there. His mouth already felt dry, but the hope of finding Ace alive and well pressed him forward.

Hours passed and his pace slowed from a light jog to a walk to a slog, dragging his feet through the sand. He felt heavier than he had ever been, weighed down by failure and regret. His stomach ached with hunger and he didn't have enough moisture in him even to lick his lips. The sand stretched into infinity around him, and his own movements seemed to be in slow motion, like he was wading through mud. He stopped for only a moment, only to shake the sand out of his shoes, but before he realized what was happening the world tilted and he collapsed on the white sands of the beach.

His head hit the ground first and he lay there in a feverish sleep for a very long time, motionless as if dead. When he awakened hours later, he was lying in front of a huge dark structure rising up out of the white sandy beach. Had this been here before he passed out, or had it appeared while he slept? Fleetingly, he hoped it might be the Tower of Views, but as he rubbed the sand out of his eyes, he saw that it was a gigantic black obelisk of some kind, half-buried in the sand and half-emerging from the sea. It looked like it had once stood proud and tall but had tipped over long ago, and now rested at a forty-five-degree angle like a ruined relic of ancient Egypt. *Look upon my works, ye mighty,* Michael thought, *and despair.*

The black obelisk seemed to stretch for miles out into the sea, and to disappear up into the clouds on the dawn horizon. On the other side, buried in the sand, its base created its own enormous dune. He stood in front of the huge black wall, and he couldn't help but be impressed at the sheer size of it. Like so many structures in this terrible Shook land, he wondered if it was built by human hands, or if it was something of a natural occurrence, born from the land itself like the mountains of Las Cruces.

Michael struggled to his feet, feeling sharply now the way his stone shoulder ground against itself, harrying his every movement. He was relieved to see the tire tracks still in the sand. They headed straight toward the obelisk and continued underneath its enormous shadow. At least he hadn't been cut-off from his only clue as to where Ace might have been taken.

He began to march toward the obelisk, following the tracks.

    HEART OF THE SPIRIT MAN

Maybe it was a marker of some kind, delineating the end of one world and the beginning of the next. Or maybe it had once been an outpost of some kind, belonging to people who dared stand up and fight against Lord Striker and his armies. As he drew nearer, he saw light reflecting off an irregularity in the sand before him. He scrambled over to the glimmer and found yet another sign, half-buried in the sand and rapidly rusting at the edges thanks to the tide. The words engraved on it struck him like a slap.

"Get it through your mortal head,

"Your spirit, man, is almost dead."

Michael wrenched the sign from the sand and hurled it into the waves with a snarl. So they knew he would follow. This was all part of some elaborate game. To what end, he didn't know, and right then, he didn't especially care. He spat at the spot where the sign had been and kept walking.

The tire tracks in the sand were all that kept him going. What else did he have to go on? Ace had to still be alive, she had to. He couldn't bring himself to consider the possibility that she'd been harmed—or, worse, that she had gone with the Strikers willingly. That latter option just wasn't possible. He had been betrayed before, but somehow, somewhere deep inside, he knew Ace would never have done such a thing. He kept himself going by telling himself that once he reached the end of the tire tracks, he'd find her. He would see her again. He knew he would.

The obelisk's immense size had made it appear much closer than it really was, and he found himself still quite a distance away from it after nearly an hour of walking. His stomach had grown so used to its hunger that it had stopped aching, but his mouth tasted disgusting, as if he'd been eating the sand of the beach. As he walked, the sand began giving way to grass, eventually resolving into a green seaside meadow full of blooming yellow and gold and deep purple flowers. Miles beyond the obelisk, he could now see, rose seven tall and majestic mountains, which towered above a carpet of deep green forest like seven angels robed in granite gowns, each trimmed with white plumes of ermine snow. Tall, crashing waterfalls splashed down their faces, and clouds wreathed their highest peaks like crowns. He looked around for some kind of sign that might tell him the name of the place, and to his surprise, he saw one. Made of two upright logs and a stone base like the park signs in New Mexico, the sign said, "Historical Marker. These mountains do not have a name because no one has ever been here before."

He shrugged and walked on, still following the tire tracks toward the obelisk. After a while he stopped in the middle of the meadow to catch his breath and rest his legs for a moment. He sat on a rock and breathed deeply. In spite of himself, he couldn't deny the beauty of this place. A bee buzzed by him and landed on a nearby flower, trading pollen for nectar in that age-old dance of life. Michael was watching the bumble bee with great interest when he heard a familiar voice behind him. He whirled around, fully expecting to see either Lord Striker or the captain ready to pounce upon him and kill him once and for all, but it was neither one of them. Instead, it was the one and only kind-hearted Wizard of Shook, Lazaro Hitchcock himself, who Michael had to admit he had begun to believe may have only been a fevered hallucination in the first place. Yet here the fine little wizard was, standing right in front of him. Lazaro's fat round face beamed with a huge smile from ear to ear and his eyes sparkled with amusement.

"Hello, my good friend from the real world," he said. "Good to see you again. How have you been?"

Michael laughed and couldn't help striding forward to wrap Lazaro in a great hug.

"I'm so glad to see you," he said, and Lazaro hugged him back, laughing. "God, Lazaro, you don't know how good it is to see your face." He pulled back and smiled down at his friend's warm face. "Things, I'll admit, have not been going exactly as I had hoped."

Lazaro eyed the stone creeping across his entire body and nodded solemnly. "Yes, I can see that," he said.

"It's not just that. I've been traveling with someone, Lazaro. Ace, she calls herself. Only, she was kidnapped just last night. I'm trying to find her."

　　　　　　　　HEART OF THE SPIRIT MAN

Lazaro raised an eyebrow. "I've never heard of her, and I know nearly everybody there is to know or not around here. Or, is she related to Solitaire, perhaps?"

"Yes, that's her," Michael said. "She said her nickname was Ace."

"I've heard her called many things," Lazaro said, stroking his fingers over his chin as if stroking an imaginary beard. "Not that, though. Some people call her Spirit Woman, if they chance to meet her. I've never had the pleasure, for I hear she doesn't have much patience for strangers. You must be very special indeed for her to have traveled with you."

Michael told Lazaro about how he and Ace had met, how ferocious she was in fighting the Strikers, how she had helped him have a vision in her house before they set off for the Tower of Views. And then, how she had vanished in the night, along with the captain and his soldiers, and how Michael had been following the tire tracks ever since.

Lazaro clucked his tongue and shook his head. "I understand the pain that you must feel, Spirit Man, but I am afraid there's nothing I can tell you about that. But listen, we don't have very much time here together, so pay attention. We live in very dangerous times right now, so I'll tell you what I know. You must go to The Garden of the Dangerous Gods and wait for a sign there."

"I'm not leaving Ace behind," Michael said.

"Believe me, you will want to receive this sign," Lazaro snapped. "It will come to you in a beautiful vision, so don't get your liver in a quiver. But before you go on to your next destination, I must give you your lesson for today. Ready? A journey of a thousand miles can be completed with a single step. If you want your heart back, you just need to know when to take that step!" He gave a huge wink and began laughing in his infectious way.

Michael just stared, exhausted and demoralized and utterly baffled by what this strange wizard was trying to tell him.

Then, as though his laughter had conjured it up, a strong gust of wind whipped up and blew across the green meadow. It raced up and down the rolling hills, parting the tall grasses and wildflowers, flattening a narrow path all the way through the green meadow and beneath the shadow of the obelisk and toward the seven majestic mountains in the far distance. Michael followed the narrow path with his eyes until it disappeared into the far horizon.

"Are you coming with me to get my heart back?" he asked Lazaro, though he knew the answer before his friend could even speak.

Lazaro shook his head and said, "No, I'm afraid I can't, Spirit Man. This is your quest. Only you can go and claim your heart back for yourself." He smiled like a well-wishing grandparent, then raised his hand in a farewell salute. "See ya later, good old buddy!"

"Wait!" Michael cried, grabbing Lazaro's arms. "You see things, you have powers. I need to know. Is...is Ace okay? Can I still save her? Please, please, I need to know!"

Lazaro's face grew serious. "Be brave, Spirit Man, be brave!"

And with that he vanished into thin air. Michael gave a wordless, angry shout and kicked a clump of dirt. What kind of an answer was that? He couldn't bring himself to believe that Ace was dead, but the idea tore at him. If she hadn't survived, if Striker's wicked army had executed her, he would have no hope against Lord Striker. If that truly was the case, he might as well give up. But no, he needed to believe, despite everything, that she was still out there. More determined than ever, he set off down the narrow path that went through the green meadow, toward the seven mountains in the distance.

He walked for what felt like weeks. His hunger and thirst seemed to level out, frozen, and though he kept expecting himself to keel over, to die of dehydration or starvation, he just kept going, his body drawing energy as if from some ethereal plane. At last, after such an arduous journey, he stepped into the shadow beneath the obelisk.

All at once, the world grew utterly silent and devoid of color. Michael turned toward the meadow he had just left and found it had become completely monochrome, as if some powerful force had simply sapped the life from every last inch of it. He tried to speak and no sound left his throat. He snapped his fingers and they made no noise at all. He kept walking, trying not to give in to the terrible sense of unease that seemed to descend from the obelisk itself. The enormous monolith loomed over him, blacker than anything he had ever seen. It reflected nothing, and instead appeared to absorb all light, like a black hole. Staring up at it, he felt that he could fall into it and vanish forever in that oblivion.

Michael kept his eyes on the mountains in the far distance, well beyond the obelisk's shadow. It wasn't so far, really. The gray sun was setting over the gray ocean. Cold, lifeless rays spilled across the land and stopped dead at the border of the shadow. It was as if he occupied a different world as he trekked beneath that enormous artifact. He could see the world he had just left from this place, but it was like looking through a thick pane of unbreakable glass, and felt so profoundly distant from where he now stood.

He detected the shapes first as a vague sensation of movement in the corners of his vision. Something not quite right, like night terrors manifesting in a pitch-dark room. Then they appeared in earnest, lanky shadows dripping tar from their half-formed bodies. They circled around him, arms dangling near the ground, loping back and forth like predators sizing up their prey. Michael paused, unsure of what to do. The figures were shaped like men, some over ten feet tall, completely black in color, their features indecipherable at a distance. Then, all at once, as if on a cue, they began sprinting toward him, racing like a night wind.

Shit. He ran too, pushing himself as hard as he could toward that edge of sunlight beyond the obelisk's shadow. As the figures drew closer, he could make out that their faces were like clay men, shapeless, featureless, horrifying. And all the while they were utterly silent, emitting not a single sound as they loped toward him like some blasphemous cross between man and beast. Michael ran as fast as he could, then pushed himself to run even harder, his panic spurring him faster than he thought he had the strength for. Still, the abominations were gaining on him, their shadowy tar trails spilling out behind them as they ran.

Michael didn't know if he was going to make it. The border between dark and light was so close now, but he could practically feel the grasping hands of these shadow creatures. He let loose a silent bellow of defiance and put every last ounce of himself into his sprint, recalling his days as a champion runner, recalling how Ace had looked as she cast shadow puppets against the rocks of their campsite. As one of the dripping things reached out to drag him back into the dark, Michael lunged with all his might. He skidded and tumbled across the line of shadow and all at once, color and sound rushed back into the world like he had thrust open a bulkhead door on a submarine.

The creatures tried to follow him, but as soon as they leapt out from beneath the obelisk and the sunlight struck them, they vaporized—just screamed noiselessly and began to vanish as the sunlight tore apart their half-formed bodies. Some of the shadow runners retreated back into the darkness that dwelt within the black wall, disappeared once more into oblivion.

Michael lay there for a while breathing hard, his legs burning as they never had before. But as soon as he was able, he scrambled to his feet and hobbled away from the obelisk as fast as his weary legs would carry him. He turned back only once, and seeing the obelisk, he felt deep within himself such a profound and primal fear at the mere shape of it, as if it somehow tapped into some lost region of his brain which knew, instinctively, to stay away. He knew he never wanted to see that black monolith ever again. He couldn't shake the thought of it as a specter of death, of utter and permanent defeat.

As he stumbled on, Michael found himself drifting in and out of waking dreams, all the exertion of the past days hitting him at once. He could not stop, could not rest, not with Ace in such danger. Yet his body was failing, threatening to collapse.

Then, from a place both deep within himself and simultaneously very, very far away, he heard a familiar voice which he knew intuitively belonged to Spirit Man.

"I will carry you," the voice said. "We will not stop. But close your eyes. Rest. Dream."

So he did, slipping into that world beyond wakefulness even as some force beyond his understanding kept his legs moving, kept his body trudging onward.

     HEART OF THE SPIRIT MAN

Michael found himself staring at a pile of gigantic red rocks which towered high into the sky. The mountains and the obelisk and the ocean were gone. A grove of California redwood trees grew in a circle around the base of these red rocks. He knew—without knowing how he knew—that this place was the Garden of the Dangerous Gods, a place sacred to those wicked gods of Shook. As he stood before the red rocks, a golden staircase descended from the sky, leading up and up and up until it disappeared into a thick blanket of silver mist and rolling fog. He could see lightning flashing in the high clouds above him and hear thunder rumbling in the far distance.

Michael hesitated for only a moment and then, with one mighty burst of pure energy, he leaped through the air and ran up the solid gold steps into the sky. His dream self had been freed of his burdens, was light as anything. He dashed up the stairs and looked down once at the earth far below. It looked so far away that he thought it seemed a long time away, too. He kept running toward the swirling, whirling clouds, where the lightning split the sky and the booming thunder shook the threads of space itself.

When he arrived on the top of the golden stairs in the sky, he stood on a small square platform, wind rushing around him and threatening to hurl him down to earth. A railing helped him brace himself, giving him something to hold onto to keep himself from being blown away. The wind howled all around him with such force that it hurt his ears. Thunder bellowed and lightning flashed across the stormy skies all around him.

A deep voice boomed from within the clouds.

"Oh, Spirit of Man, are you ready to be tested by the fire? Tell me why you have come so far in your journey, even when all has been lost from the beginning of time."

"Because I'm a stubborn son of a bitch," Michael shouted back at the spirit of the wind. "I don't care what the fates say. I'm not giving up."

"But it is already too late," cried out the spirit of the wind. "You lost this battle before you were even born. If you proceed, you will not prevent suffering, you will not prevent death, you will only sentence far more people to it."

With a howl and a moan, the spirit's voice swept the clouds away from the sky above him. Michael looked up in utter awe as the sky itself opened up and peeled back, revealing a huge black hole in space above him. Then the hole began to grow smaller and smaller, and to rush down toward Michael, as though the sky had folded itself down to create a periscope pointing right at him.

Then from the depths and darkness of the black hole, he heard a voice, a woman's voice, faint and distant.

"Michael?" the voice called out. "Michael, can you hear me?"

"Ace!" Michael cried.

"Michael, listen, 1 know you're on a whole quest right now, but just remember that you can't save anyone if you can't save yourself. When the time comes, you will know what to do. 1 know you will. But Michael, listen closely, don't forget—"

The wind's howling rose and swept away the echoes of Ace's voice.

There was a moment of silence, then a lightning bolt exploded, splitting the platform in half. The pieces fell away like a demolished golden skyscraper, and for an instant Michael hung in the air. Then he fell.

Michael came to and found himself standing alone in the dazzling light of a new day on the shores of an island he had never seen before. Terminal Island, he somehow knew. But how? Behind him whispered the gentle waves of a blood red sea. He looked up and down the shore, filled with hope that he would see Ace come running up to meet him. But there was nothing, just another lonely landscape, another horizon, another path, another invitation to nowhere. And there it was, not too far away, a white marble spire atop a wooded hill: the Tower of Views. It was tall and graceful, tapering to a sharp point at the top, which was capped with gold that gleamed like an eye. As though it had been made just for him, the path on which he stood led directly to it.

Okay. This was it. He took a deep breath. Was he choosing the path or was the path choosing him? Had Spirit Man found a way to this

          HEART OF THE SPIRIT MAN

island, or had someone else reached out and brought them here? Well, whatever the case, there was only one way forward now, and it lay clear as day before him.

He followed the narrow path up to the Tower of Views, where he found no entrance of any kind, no door, only smooth white marble. Of course. Before it stood a small, elegant wooden plaque, mounted on an eight-foot replica of the tower itself. Michael read it, sighed softly, and smiled.

*"Welcome, Traveler, to
the Tower of Views
where we all wind up
eventually."*

Chapter 13

Michael Seymour, Spirit Man, Dreamer of Worlds, stood before the shining pillar known as the Tower of Views and reached out a hand to touch its cool stone. A great rumble, like a giant beast awakening, emerged from beneath the ground, and Michael stepped back instinctively as the smooth surface of the tower began to split in two before him. A pair of gold-trimmed glass doors, at least fifteen feet tall, revealed themselves. Bizarrely, there appeared to be an inner tower hidden by the outer layer, slightly narrower but just as tall. A gust of cold wind rolled around Michael but he didn't even flinch. More of him was stone now than flesh. Time was nearly up. As if in response to this thought, chimes sounded in the distance, tinny and frantic. A memory seized him, of standing on his parents' porch as a child, watching great black thunder clouds gathering behind the Organ mountains, their teeth seeming to tear chunks from the storm, the wind chimes on the porch jangling madly as great stormy gusts washed past.

The Tower had been waiting for him here, and it felt rude to keep it waiting. Michael steeled himself for whatever might wait inside and stepped forward, pushing the doors open and walking through them. Snowflakes began to swirl out from the doors, washing over Spirit Man, engulfing him in cold as he entered. The doors swung shut behind him, leaving him in a great hallway.

The hallway was ten, maybe twenty stories high, its smooth walls rising to a lofty domed ceiling, all in a shimmery pearly gray, as though the tower had not been built, but had grown like a pearl inside an oyster. A wide path of gold-streaked white marble went all the way through the hallway. On one side of the white marble path grew a rich green forest of oaks and tall pine trees and golden aspens. Some were so old and tall that they almost touched the top of the dome, their bases at least ten feet across, and Michael felt like a dwarf standing under them. It was like being Little Red Riding Hood, standing in front of a great, primordial forest and feeling tiny, fragile, easily devoured by the things that lurked in the dark. Thick black vines grew along the gray walls of the great hallway, climbing and snaking all the way up to the top of the domed ceiling. Some of these vines also grew along the overhanging branches of the great oaks and tall pine trees and golden aspens, like long slender black snakes dangling from the huge branches above his head.

But on the other side of the white marble path, nothing grew at all. Everything looked like it had been dead for hundreds of years, black and burnt. Among the ashes, he thought he saw shapes that could be bones, skulls heaped under the soot, but when he blinked, the shapes shifted and reformed, leaving him uncertain of what he saw.

It hit him suddenly, striking fear through him. This was the Garden of Two Deaths. The life bursting on one side, springing up to the ceiling even as the dark vines reached down, and the death on the other, remnants of life still buried within. That had to be where he was. And if he was right about that, then he was in tremendous peril.

For a moment, Michael felt the fear well up within him again, spreading outward from the heavy stone in his chest. He almost turned around to see if the door had closed behind him, if there was still a chance to turn back and try his luck in another world instead, not this place of ash and bone. But Spirit Man closed his eyes and gathered his courage.

"There is nothing to fear," he said to himself. "If death comes, it comes. It if does not, I prevail."

He could only imagine what Ace would think if she caught him thinking about turning around. "Get your butt in gear, sweetheart," she would probably say. "This is no time to be second-guessing ourselves." So he continued walking forward, the garden of life and death on either side.

Then he walked around a corner of the white marble path and froze dead in his tracks. His eyes widened, his hands began to tremble. His chest felt as cold and empty as a great stone cave, a chasm of stone and nothingness. Before him lay a huge glass room, like a greenhouse in the shape of a tall jar. It was several stories high, surrounded on all sides by a mossy grotto ripe with life so rich and so flourishing, he couldn't conceive of it having any connection to Lord Striker. But wrapped within the vines, half-buried in the bark of trees, blooming in the center of beautiful flowers, he saw fleshy red masses of muscle. Hearts, still bloody, powering the whole wretched greenhouse. Bile rose in his throat and it was all he could do to keep from vomiting, covering his mouth with his hand even as he stepped into the room. After the nausea passed, he lifted his palm to touch one of the hearts. It was still beating and still warm, heat radiating from within it. How could all these people, all these hearts, end up in this godforsaken tower? The shock was beginning to pass, now, and he wondered at the sight of all those hearts, wrapped in their cocoons of greenery. Of all the strange things he'd seen in his journeys through the worlds, this was the most painful to view. Each heart, a person's chest left empty. Each heart, a life ripped away. How terrible for the people of Shook, to be robbed of such a crucial thing with violence and such cruelty.

He knew only one thing for certain, and that was that Lord Striker had to be nearby. There was no way that such a vainglorious god would leave his prizes, his ultimate shrine to his own power and glory, alone for very long. The murderer of his own people would surely need to keep the reminders of his own evil close to hand.

"Bastard," Michael growled under his breath.

Just then, a sharp explosion and a crackling cloud of purple smoke appeared right in front of him, hovering just over the ground. Michael jumped back and the cloud expanded, forcing him to continue backpedaling. The explosion echoed in loud peals from the walls of gray pearl, and the sound vibrated throughout the long and winding chambers of the Tower of Views. A moment later, Lord Striker emerged from the cloud and stood before Michael, draped in his royal blue robe and towering over his prey. Michael did not move an inch or twitch a muscle. His stomach seemed to drop away, but he kept his expression cool, meeting Striker's eyes with

   HEART OF THE SPIRIT MAN

a level gaze of his own. *Nothing to fear, nothing to fear*, he reminded himself, and he tilted his chin back silently in a wordless challenge. Let this god of storms and destruction be the one on the defensive.

"So, you've arrived, Spirit Man," Lord Striker said with a rumbling laugh. "I was not certain you'd make it, though I'm pleased to see you defy my expectations. Good for you. Congratulations." He spread his hands out wide in a mockery of welcome. "You have found my secret holy place, Spirit Man, and you have also found me. Welcome, dear friend, to my Tower of Views, where no one of mortal skin and bone has ever stepped foot before. You should be proud of yourself! Though you aren't exactly skin and bone anymore, are you?"

With a wave to follow him, Lord Striker turned and began to walk along the wide marble path. "Come," he said, "before I must kill you, let me show you what this is all for."

"And why should I go with you?" Michael demanded. "Who are you to tell me to go anywhere?"

Lord Striker paused and looked back at Michael with an inscrutable expression. "There is no reason for anything, Spirit Man," he said. "Not even for gods. But if you must have one, let it be this: I can kill you now, or later. If you'll indulge me for a moment, we can postpone the violence."

He turned and again began to walk along the path. After a moment's consideration, Michael followed after him, keeping a safe distance between them and casting his eyes about for anything he might use as a weapon.

Lord Striker did not so much as glance back as he walked, apparently confident that nothing Michael could throw at him would do any real damage. They left behind the greenhouse of hearts and continued along the marble hallway, the living and dead forest still on either side of the path. Many more huge glass doors, leading to more greenhouses filled with hearts, flanked the hall. Now and then, a few animals or birds darted through the thick of the living forest, and Michael saw that many of them had hearts growing out of parts of their body like tumors. The ashes and soot on the dead side of the path remained unstirred, motionless. There were hearts on that side as well, though they were blackened by fire, shriveled and unbeating.

Somehow, Michael could not believe all the people to whom those hearts had once belonged were dead. If he had learned anything, wasn't it that you could kill a person, but not their spirit? Not their true heart? Then again, his entire left arm had by this point turned to stone, fingers and all. He could flex them still, but it took effort, and he was certain that before long the whole arm would freeze, like the arm of a statue.

The path snaked under hanging black vines, green leaves growing from their coiling length. Lord Striker walked through them as if they weren't there, ignoring them as they caught on his cloak, in his hair.

It seemed like they had been walking for hours, Lord Striker always a few paces ahead of Michael, when they finally came to the end of the white marble path. They stopped at the edge of a circle of green grass, perhaps ten feet in diameter. In the middle of it was a white circular stone altar.

"Come," said Lord Striker, beckoning. "Look. Look upon your people." He gestured to the altar on the grass.

Hesitantly, Michael walked to the altar. The top was a perfectly polished, perfectly smooth disc of stone. At first, he thought it was reflecting light in peculiar ways, but when he looked closer, he realized he could see images within the stone, moving as if on a screen. Somewhere in Shook, perhaps near or perhaps far, a crowd of people had gathered in a parched field. There were perhaps ten thousand of them, maybe more, all huddled close together and pressing up against one another so that they seemed like one moving mass. They were dressed in brown robes, with very long and unkempt hair, and their faces were dirty and sweaty, some tear-streaked. Some in the crowd were half-naked, their ribs sticking out in sharp contrast to the hollows of their bellies.

Each person had a light brown basket made from Yucca plants and all of their baskets were empty. Each had a black band tightly squeezed around their neck which, as far as Michael could tell,

   HEART OF THE SPIRIT MAN

prevented them from speaking or muttering a word at all. Despite how many of them there were, the only sounds Michael could hear through the stone were low grunts of pain, animal sounds of hurt and anger.

Then a man wearing a white mask appeared, riding upon a white horse. He was dressed in a long and loosely fitting white robe which flowed freely in the wind as he rode through the middle of the field. The horseman rode around like a hero in his glory, and the people swarmed around him. On the sides of the horse were large saddlebags, from which he began to pull out long loaves of bread. He tore each one into pieces, and threw the pieces into the crowd. Then he took out two large smoked fish, and he began to tear them into pieces, and to throw pieces of the oily flesh to the people. Croaking and groaning, they held up their baskets, trying to catch a piece of bread or fish.

"He comes each day to feed the thousands of hungry and poor basket weavers," Lord Striker said. "See how his efforts change the world!" He forced a bitter laugh.

Michael watched the rider with the white mask ride in, throw food in all directions, and then leave again, just as he had come. After the horseman rode off into the setting sun, the people looked into their baskets and found them as empty as before, letting out low animal whines of sadness.

"I don't understand," Michael said.

"Ah, but I think you do. This is but one scene of Shook. There are many like it. Huddled, hungry masses crying out for help and receiving none. Tell me, Spirit Man, how many people have you saved, here in Shook? How many towns and villages?"

"I don't know."

"And have you ever considered that for every one you save, there are a thousand more whom you will not save? Whom you will not help? I believed, once, that I could do all that was required, that I could make Shook a beautiful place through my own deeds, roaming from town to town, village to village."

Lord Striker then strode over to the white stone altar and ran his hand across the polished surface. As he moved his clawed hand, the image changed rapidly from one scene to another, all depicting unimaginable suffering.

"I understand now that this can never be. That to truly end suffering, one must take more...drastic action."

Michael looked up at him and felt for the first time that he truly saw Lord Striker as he was. Not an invincible god, but a simple madman, driven to insanity by trying to attain the unattainable.

"So you inflict it," he said. "You kill and you maim, and for what? How will that end suffering, in your estimation?"

"It's quite simple, really. I need them to stop hoping." He again slid his hand across the stone and returned to the field of the basket people. "You see them? Still keening, still begging, still hoping. They believe that something will change. They believe that tomorrow, when the horseman comes, he will bring more food. They believe that tomorrow the food will not disappear the moment it leaves their baskets. The mothers and fathers believe their children will grow up to be big and strong enough to escape this pitiful, destitute existence. The children believe they will be chosen by the horseman to ride away with him on the back of his steed. They all believe that someday soon the rains will come again and their crops will grow again and everything, everything, will be better. No matter how many days or weeks or months or years pass in which none of these things occur, they go right on believing that tomorrow, tomorrow will be different.

"And so they suffer. And so they will suffer for eternity. And so all of Shook suffers thus. But you see, Spirit Man, it is not an unsolvable problem. Suffering is inevitable, this much is true. I fought against this for eons, since the world itself was born. I raged against the universe, tried to do battle with this unchangeable fact. But even I, even I was powerless against it. So, let me ask you: If suffering is inevitable, unchangeable, what then are we to do? We, who wish to create a perfect world."

Michael did not answer. He knew where Lord Striker was going and couldn't bring himself to say the words aloud.

   HEART OF THE SPIRIT MAN

"I will tell you," said Lord Striker. "All that is left to us is to remove hope. Because it is the hope that makes the suffering painful. All these dreams of a better life. If I can shake these dreams from the people of Shook, then there shall be no more pain. If I can force them to accept that life is brutal, violent, and short, there shall be no more pain. If I can make them understand that, at any moment, their son may be slain, their town burned to ash, their heart ripped from their chest and planted in my garden, there shall be no more pain. Don't you understand? Think of the people of Gehenna, who understand that their lot in life is to suffer unimaginably, to have their entrails torn out by hungry dogs and nailed to the ceiling, to cut the throat of their comrade and have theirs cut in turn, to bleed to death only to wake the next morning with more blood that will be spilled once more by nightfall. All this is horror, is it not? Yet their lives are immeasurably better than those of the basket people. I mean, just look at them down there, dreaming of all these things which will never come to pass. They are pathetic. If all lives looked like those of the tortured souls of Gehenna, then Shook would truly be a paradise."

Michael realized with a start that Lord Striker actually wanted—no, he needed—Michael to agree with him. He needed someone to say that what he was doing was right and just. Michael only shook his head.

"You're insane," he said. "You lost your mind so long ago, you don't even realize anymore that it left you."

Lord Striker shrank back, genuinely wounded. He quickly recovered, however, and stood to his full, domineering height.

"Very well," he said. "If you will not see reason, we have nothing further to discuss."

"Time for violence, then?"

"Nearly."

Lord Striker snapped his fingers and a crystal decanter materialized atop the stone altar.

"I believe you are after this," he said.

Inside floated Michael's heart. It had been so long since he had seen it that he almost didn't believe it was truly his when he first saw it. But something about the way it beat, the rhythm of that contraction, told him it was his. It could be no one else's.

"Were you going to plant this in your garden, then?" Michael said. "Grow a poplar tree around it? Maybe a weeping willow." Michael had to resist the urge to grab his heart instantly, smash his fist through the glass and seize it back. He had been needing it for so long, his chest had felt so empty for ages now, and here it was before him. This, this was what the entire quest had been for, and it was as if he could see Ace's hands on the top of the jar, waiting for him to lift away the barrier so she could raise it up to him. His stone hand itched but he held it steady.

"No, as a matter of fact," Lord Striker said. "I had no intention of planting this one in my garden. It is far too valuable."

"Then what? What was it all for? Why did you need my heart at all?"

Lord Striker clicked his tongue and paused as if deciding whether or not to tell Michael the truth. Then he shrugged his enormous shoulders as if to ask, "Why not?" and reached one huge hand up toward his neck. He pulled one side of his robe away from his chest to reveal a burned, blackened scar in the flesh, right above where his heart would have been. Black veins of corruption extended from the spot, reaching all over his thickly muscled form like a poison.

"I thought I might take it for myself," he said. "Mine has been of no use to me for quite a long time now. I wanted to remember what it is like to feel."

Michael didn't know what to say. He looked down at his own chest, stony and impenetrable as it was. Lazaro had been right after all. They weren't so different, he and Lord Striker, and that thought terrified him. He shook it off.

"It wouldn't beat for you," Michael said. "Not in a million years."

"Yes, well," Lord Striker said. "We will see."

With one swift motion, he shattered the decanter against the altar and snatched the heart in his massive hand. Michael cried out and lunged forward but Lord Striker sent him hurtling backward with a vicious kick. Michael crashed into the marble wall and staggered to his feet, but something was wrong. His limbs weren't quite obeying him, were rapidly slowing in their movements.

"I am sorry, Spirit Man, in a way," Lord Striker said. "But I couldn't take any chances. When we met on a mountaintop, I whispered a command to that stone in your chest, and now I'm afraid I must instruct it to act on that command." He snapped his fingers and all at once a tremendous pain shot through Michael's entire body. He screamed and looked down to see everything rapidly turning to stone, the transformation accelerating far beyond his control. His legs turned first, rooting him in place, then his arms, frozen now by his sides. Last, the stone began to creep up his neck, then his jaw, inches from turning him now and forever into a statue. The Second Death.

Lord Striker shook his head with what appeared to be genuine sadness and peeled open his own chest. In the dark space behind his ribs, Michael saw only shriveled blackness, no heart at all.

"Farewell, Michael Seymour, Spirit Man, whatever you choose to call yourself. I hope you find peace in death, as so few ever do."

Lord Striker moved to place Michael's heart in his own chest and then time ground to a halt. It was as if the gears of the world simply jammed. Michael could see, but couldn't even blink. Lord Striker was frozen mid-movement, the heart only inches from his chest. A strange mist filled the room, and within it, Michael heard a familiar voice.

"You're not getting away from me that easily, sweetheart."

He tried to speak, but could not.

"Shh, don't worry, you don't have to say a thing." Ace, only half-present, shimmering like she, too, was made of mist, stepped out of the fog and stood before him. She wore a starry robe of purples and blues, scattered with sparkles of the stars that seemed to move as if in a real galaxy. Her hair was swept back from her face and her eyes were rimmed in kohl, making them seem huge and dark as night. "You're not finished yet, you know. Do you remember what Lazaro said?"

One step, he thought. *One step can cover a thousand miles.*

"That's right. And just like I said, you'll know what to do when the time comes. Well, the time is now, Spirit Man."

The mist dissipated and time began creaking back to its usual pace, yet Ace remained, ethereal and ghostly before him. Lord Striker seemed not to have noticed anything, so enraptured was he by the prospect of regaining a heart after so very, very long. Michael knew he had only a single instant to act, and he would have to fight against this stone prison to do so. He looked at Ace. She met his gaze. Then she smiled and nodded.

With a single step, exerting the last of his strength against the stone, Michael stepped not toward his own heart, but toward Ace. He embraced her and kissed her deeply even as the stone crept up to his lips. She kissed him back and in spite of everything it seemed that, in that moment, all was right with the world.

A shockwave exploded through the marble tower. Lord Striker stopped and looked up, confused. The shockwave was followed by another, then another. They sent cracks rippling through the marble walls and debris tumbling to the floor. The domed ceiling cracked wide open and split in half, and rays of sunlight burst through the opening. The shockwaves came again. Thump-thump. Thump-thump. They were emanating from Michael's heart!

The shockwaves grew so intense that they shattered the stone encasing Michael. Fragments of it crashed to the floor, revealing the living skin beneath. He held Ace even tighter and laughed, delighting in the chaos caused by this one, simple act of love.

The next shockwave was too strong even for Lord Striker, and he lost his grip on the heart. It began tumbling toward the floor and Michael cried out, realizing he wouldn't reach it in time. But then, just before that precious organ collided with the cold, hard marble, Ace dove and caught it with both hands. She looked up at Michael and grinned.

"Gotcha," she said.

Lord Striker howled with rage as everything he had built came crashing down around him. With one final, searing look at Michael and Ace, he whirled around and disappeared into nothingness, transporting himself to some distant world to lick his wounds.

Another wave of shocks tore through the tower, and all the walls in the great hallway began to split apart, huge chunks of marble falling down all around them. Ace put one hand on Michael's shoulder and offered his heart with the other. He wrapped his hand around the beating organ and they both stood like that, holding the exposed heart, looking into each other's eyes. An archway supporting the ceiling crashed down beside them and shattered into a thousand pieces.

"Spirit Man," Ace said. "Listen to me. I don't have much time." Even as she spoke, she seemed to waver, as intangible as an oasis in a desert.

"What are you talking about?"

"I wish I could go back with you, back to your world, but I'm as much a part of this place as it is a part of me, and it's not my time. I cannot walk as you do, not yet. I am not bound by the same rules, just as you are not bound by mine." The mist that comprised her form was dissipating, he felt her growing insubstantial in his arms.

"No, Ace," he said. "Please. You can. You can come with me."

"Oh, my sweet Spirit Man. Please remember that nothing ever ends, not for you. We'll meet again, somewhere, somehow." She reached out a hand as if to stroke his cheek but it passed straight through him. He tried to take her hand and his closed on empty air.

"See you around, Spirit Man," she said. And then she was gone.

Michael fell to his knees, cradling his heart against his chest. The entire tower was collapsing around him but he couldn't care less in that moment. How could she go? After everything, how could she go? Yet at the same time, he knew that what she had said was true. They would meet again, he was sure of it. Their two souls, their two spirits, were woven together in the tapestry of the universe. They might drift apart for a while, but they could never truly be separated.

"I will find you," he said. "I will."

Then the floor gave way beneath him and he was falling again, tumbling through a gap between the worlds. Huge slabs of stone and white marble and gold and trees fell down with him, tumbling and twisting in the void. Michael went spiraling down, down, down through space and time itself. He fell through a world of darkness with tiny patches of twinkling stars in a distant galaxy and he knew beyond any doubt that each star had a planet just like his own, people with hearts walking on them just like upon his own. His body was spinning out of control but he was still somehow able to hold onto the heart in his hands, through a massive effort of will. Then there was a blinding flash of light and everything went away.

A kaleidoscope of colors unfurled in Spirit Man's closed eyelids

Chapter 14

as he waited for the world to settle around him. Where would he be now? His heart pounded in his hands and he slowly, slowly opened his eyes, unsure of what he would find before him.

The full moon shone brightly above the rugged peaks of the Organ Mountains of southern New Mexico as if it had been poised there, waiting for his return. He stood and found himself standing in a clearing on top of Mount Solitaire, surrounded by dark pines. The enormous stone pillar had vanished but everything else was just as he had left it. He stood still, cautious, for several long moments, still holding the heart in his hands and expecting Lord Striker to appear at any second.

Then, once he was sure he was not about to be ambushed, he looked down, knowing what he would see. The body of Michael Seymour was splayed grotesquely on the ground. His chest was spread open, revealing a gaping emptiness inside where sat a hunk of yellow stone instead of a heart.

A breeze drifted over the desert, cool, almost refreshing. The night was quiet, peaceful. Spirit Man sighed at the sight of the gaping hole, the yellow stone within, as if a rock could ever take the place of a real heart. A strange sensation of loneliness swept over him, though he couldn't say where it emerged from. Somehow all of the bizarre and horrifying things that had happened to him in the many spirit worlds he had visited seemed to be very small at that moment, faced with the wounded shape before him. He wanted nothing more than to reach down and protect himself, shelter himself from the world and its viciousness.

Spirit Man shifted his focus to the gently beating heart in his hand.

"Through all this, you're still beating," he said softly, fondly, like talking to a dear friend. "Through these worlds, you're still going on." Carefully, almost reverently, he cupped the heart in both hands. It pulsed steadily, dripping live red blood through his fingers and upon the parched earth below. Spirit Man drew the heart back down to his own chest, closing his eyes as if trying to hear a distant rhythm. After a moment of contemplation, he knelt down next to the lifeless body. He took the yellow stone from that cavity and tossed it aside, not caring where it landed. What was a simple stone next to the miracle of a human heart?

Then he leaned in close and whispered, "Thank you, Michael," in the man's ear. And he gently placed the heart, ever beating, back into Michael's chest.

Michael Seymour's eyes snapped open, and he gasped like a man startled from sleep. He found himself looking straight into the eyes of…well, of himself. An older, wiser version of himself, with stars in his eyes and streaks of snowy white through his hair. For perhaps only a fraction of a second, Michael Seymour the man and Spirit Man were both one person and two people, and Michael could not tell who was doing the thinking, and who was looking at whom. His consciousness felt at once split and united, divided and whole.

He started to say something, perhaps to ask something, but Spirit Man touched his lips with a finger.

"Your heart returns, my friend," Spirit Man said. "So you must return to your world, and I to mine." He smiled, and Michael had never seen something as unnerving or as joyful as his own smile reflected back to him from another person. "For the moment, at least."

As Michael's sense of being himself began to return, he saw his spirit counterpart as something like an identical twin, but shining with the warmth and wisdom of the most ancient grandfather.

"What are you going to do?" he said. "Will you be okay?"

Spirit Man laughed. "Oh, Michael, how very like you, to ask after me before you know your own fate." He looked so joyful in the moonlight. "I might spend some more infinity with Lazaro Hitchcock. I might see if Lord Striker wants to arm wrestle. I might make certain that Spirit Woman made it home okay." Michael's heart thudded in his chest. How could he have forgotten how painful, how

     HEART OF THE SPIRIT MAN

wonderful, it was to have a heart?

"Will you tell Ace something?" Michael asked.

Spirit Man gave a single nod.

Michael considered for a second, then weakly waved his hand. "Actually, never mind. I'm pretty sure she already knows." In fact he was more sure of this than anything that had happened to him so far. He could hear her voice in his head, calling him sweetheart, teasing him, and he knew that they hadn't said their final goodbyes. The universe abhorred a vacuum, as his father had always said, and without Ace, there was a void in him that could never be filled. What use was a Spirit Man without a Spirit Woman?

It was odd—he'd known her for such a short time, yet he felt that, to the contrary, he had known her since long before he was even born.

Spirit Man asked, "My friend, what will you do from here?"

"I'm going to be glad I'm alive, first of all," Michael said. But he had to ask one more question, perhaps the most important. "I have to know: was I dreaming?"

Spirit Man's face went solemn like a cloud passing over the moon. "Alive and well you are, my dear friend, but you have not been dreaming. It has been much more than that. Saying that is not to deny the importance of having a dream, which is also much more than just dreaming. I learned a million or a billion worlds ago that life is a temporary vessel for the eternal spirit, the substance of wonderful new dreams come true. I also had to learn that it is made up of the shards of old broken dreams, of mistakes, and disappointments, and tragedy.

"The real world is just as shaky as Shook, and in the fullness of time, all things here will surely pass away, just as the worlds you visited there have vanished with the sunrise. Nothing lasts, Michael, and in the end of all things, we have left only ourselves, and our dreams, for they are not of the world at all, but of the Spirit."

Spirit Man smiled, looking ancient and youthful all at once. He reached forward and pressed the palm of his hand against Michael's now-healed chest, where a heart pounded beneath. "Do your best to keep that thing shut from now on, all right, my friend? But not too shut."

A great humming sound began to swell up around them, and Spirit Man looked to the moonlit sky.

"Oh, I guess that's my signal," he said. He stood up and turned around to see a pair of huge silvery arches rise up out of the desert as if they were bones emerging from the dust. The sound was coming from them as though they were a pair of huge tuning forks, ringing a deep and melodious note. Spirit Man turned back to extend a hand to Michael and helped him to his feet. "I'm going to the City of Arches first, my friend. Do you wish to follow behind?"

Michael grinned and shook his head. "Thanks, Spirit Man, but I think I'd better stick around here for a while. I've been away long enough." He looked toward the hospital, a strange feeling passing over to him. The world seemed at once as familiar as his childhood home and as strange as any world he'd visited. How was he to grow accustomed again to this place that was supposed to be his?

Spirit Man nodded his head in understanding and agreement. "Suit yourself, my friend," he said. "If you need me, you know where to find me."

"I guess I do," Michael said.

The full moon touched the horizon, shining directly through the great arches. Spirit Man gave Michael a small wave, turned toward that silver glow, and was gone. In the east, the first gray light of dawn had begun to creep across the horizon.

Michael turned his gaze toward the Land of Enchantment. The city of Las Cruces was only just beginning to awaken, a few cars moving along the roads, street sweepers crawling along the curb. There was a sense of fragility in the pre-dawn morning. So many people emerging into the world, not knowing what they would find when they arrived. It was beautiful, really. The uncertainty of it all. Because everyone got up and went about their days anyway, even knowing that at any moment, something truly terrible could happen. They went about their days with hope in their hearts, believing— really believing—that good things awaited them.

Dawn broke as Michael jogged down the mountain, through the scrub bushes of creosote and mesquite and the tall stalks of yucca. His heart beat stronger than ever before. It felt new and bright as a bird in his chest, and it struck him as wildly strange that he'd never taken the time before to just appreciate its beating, its careful and joyous rhythm.

He wondered how long had he been away. Twenty seconds? Twenty years? Or had no time at all gone by? He really didn't have a clue, and he leaped and danced higher, and yelling louder as he recognized that didn't matter to him one bit. He knew only that he was right there right then and glad to be back home in New Mexico, and his heart was alive and full of love. He swung his arms in wide full circles, dropped into bouncing deep knee bends like a ballet dancer, then leaped straight up into the air, landed on his feet, and continued running like a young deer, uncaring of the future or the past because what mattered was now, now, now and the joy of the run. Cool wind rushed past him and he felt it on every inch of his body, felt it on every hair along his arms and his legs. He reveled in the novelty of sensation as if he had only just been born. As he ran he leaned over and ran his hand across the scrub. He bent down and scooped up a handful of dirt and let it slide through his fingers, marveling at its smoothness against his palm. Gone was the stone skin, gone was the distance from the living world. Everything was here and immediate and he could touch it, could really touch it.

Michael ran up a steep sandy hill and then he ran swiftly down the other side, pumping his legs as fast as they would go. How could he have ever forgotten what a joy it was simply to run? How could a stone heart have ever robbed him of this? He sprinted down a meandering arroyo like a slalom skier, throwing plumes of sand out to both sides. He bounded from granite boulder to boulder like a circus gymnast on a field of beach ball trampolines. Then his surging new heart was doubly charged with power when he emerged atop a rise and saw the sunset in full bloom before him. Its burning rays sliced through a grove of tall cottonwood trees and slashed across the desert where already little lizards were receiving the signal that the day had begun and it was time to rouse themselves, where quail cheeped and jaybirds chirped, where an entire invisible crust of hidden life stretched out for miles and miles across the land, which was not nearly so barren as it appeared to the untrained eye. Red and gold rays spilled across it all, setting the sandy soil aflame. In the distance, the mountains were returning to life as the light washed over their stern and stoic faces. The deep-shadowed folds between those great rocky towers only emphasized further the glow that was spreading across them. It was nothing which could be captured by a camera, nothing which Michael could ever explain to anyone in this world or the next. It was something which could only be witnessed here, now, in this very moment which he occupied. He was so fortunate, he understood now, so very fortunate just to see a simple thing like this unfold. And he would see it again tomorrow, and the next day, and the next. He would not forget.

As he ran and his heart pounded, memories from Shook ran with him, reminding him that no matter what he did, he could never forget what had happened there. The bodies in the town the Strikers destroyed, the beauty of the City of Rocks, the stars spinning above and the emptiness in his chest. He thought of the wizard Lazaro, his bouncing joy and inscrutable riddles, his "humble" castle of feast and sleep. He thought of Lord Striker and his great clawed hands, his booming voice, his ravaged heart and his sorrow.

And most importantly, most of all, he thought of Ace, the way she crinkled her nose when she smiled, the way she always seemed to know just a little bit more than he did, the playful promise in her voice when she told him they would meet again. Spirit Woman. Was there an Ace out in the real world, just as there was a Michael? He didn't understand, not a bit, who she was or where she came from, but the stirring in his heart told him that she was far from imaginary, and his journey with her was far from over. He laid his hand over his chest, and slowed his run to a jog, listened to the slowing rhythm of his heart. Wherever she was, whatever she was doing, all he could do was hope that Ace was happy, and that their fates would intertwine again. He'd see her everywhere now, he knew this as surely as he knew that the sun would rise and that dreams were meant to shake the world.

In the distance, beyond the reach of the desert, stood the hospital. And somewhere within lay Michael's real body, intact and healthy once more, ready to take on the world. Michael ran straight toward it. Bathed in the light of a fragile, irreplaceable morning, he ran and ran.

ABOUT THE AUTHOR
George Mendoza

George Mendoza was born in New York City in 1955. At the age of 15, he was diagnosed with a rare, incurable, degenerative eye disease, fundus flavimaculatus. Effects of the disease caused him to lose his central vision, keeping only a gray foggy fringe on the periphery. In the center of 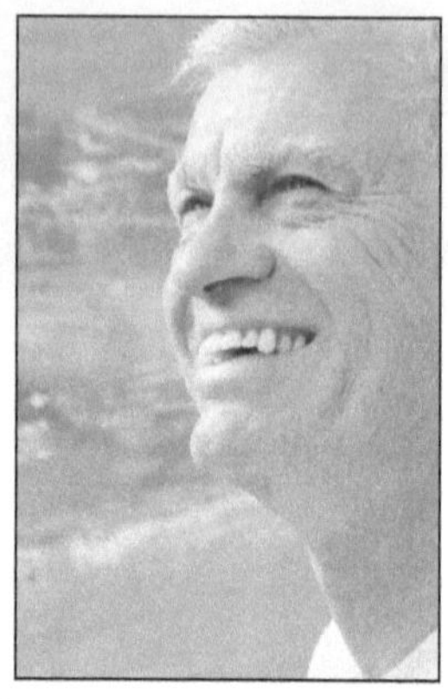 his view, he sees what he calls "kaleidoscope eyes"— intense and changing visual images of fiery suns, brightly burning eyes; and colorful pinwheels. These spectacles almost never leave him, not even when he lays down in darkness to go to sleep.

A man of vision and courage, George went on to become a world-class runner and Paralympic contender. In 1980, he broke the world record for blind athletes, running the mile in 4 minutes and 28 seconds. In the early 1990's, he began to paint full-time. Ironically, Mendoza's paintings spring from the loss of his eyesight and a very special vision that took its place. He had grown increasingly frustrated by his dancing colors, which would not leave him alone. He spoke to a priest at the Holy Cross Retreat House in New Mexico. "Paint them," the priest said. "Make designs, pictures from them."

George Mendoza remembers physical sight, and so his works derive from visual memories intertwined with dreams, visions, and emotional experiences, meaning Mendoza paints both figuratively and abstractly. His work then transcends the physical world, exploring the spiritual, the mystical, the playful, and sometimes the darker nuances of the human spirit.

Mendoza works full time as a writer and an artist. Currently, his exhibition "Colors of the Wind" is a national Smithsonian affiliates traveling art exhibit. He lives in Las Cruces, New Mexico, and is founder and president of the Wise Tree Foundation, Inc., a non-profit corporation for the promotion for the arts. He is a motivational speaker and is currently developing a play based on his children's book *Colors of the Wind*, a biography of his life written by J.L. Powers and illustrated using Mendoza's artwork.

Learn more at www.georgemendoza.com.